Praise for Andrea Camilleri
and the Montalbano Series

"Camilleri's Inspector Montalbano mysteries might sell like hotcakes in Europe, but these world-weary crime stories were unknown here until the oversight was corrected (in Stephen Sartarelli's salty translation) by the welcome publication of *The Shape of Water*. . . . This savagely funny police procedural . . . prove[s] that sardonic laughter is a sound that translates ever so smoothly into English." —*The New York Times Book Review*

"Hailing from the land of Umberto Eco and La Cosa Nostra, Montalbano can discuss a pointy-headed book like *Western Attitudes Toward Death* as unflinchingly as he can pore over crime-scene snuff photos. He throws together an extemporaneous lunch of shrimp with lemon wedges and oil as gracefully as he dodges advances from attractive women." —*Los Angeles Times*

"[Camilleri's mysteries] offer quirky characters, crisp dialogue, bright storytelling—and Salvo Montalbano, one of the most engaging protagonists in detective fiction. . . . Montalbano is a delightful creation, an honest man on Sicily's mean streets." —*USA Today*

"Camilleri is as crafty and charming a writer as his protagonist is an investigator." —*The Washington Post Book World*

"Like Mike Hammer or Sam Spade, Montalbano is the kind of guy who can't stay out of trouble. . . . Still, deftly and lovingly translated by Stephen Sartarelli, Camilleri makes it abundantly clear that under the gruff, sardonic exterior our inspector has a heart of gold, and that any outbursts, fumbles, or threats are made only in the name of pursuing truth." —*The Nation*

"Camilleri can do a character's whole backstory in half a paragraph." —*The New Yorker*

"Subtle, sardonic, and *molto simpatico*: Montalbano is the Latin re-creation of Philip Marlowe, working in a place that manages to be both more and less civilized than Chandler's Los Angeles." —*Kirkus Reviews* (starred review)

"Wit and delicacy and the fast-cut timing of farce play across the surface . . . but what keeps it from frothing into mere intellectual charm is the persistent, often sexually bemused Montalbano, moving with ease along zigzags created for him, teasing out threads of discrepancy that unravel the whole." —*Houston Chronicle*

"Sublime and darkly humorous . . . Camilleri balances his hero's personal and professional challenges perfectly and leaves the reader eager for more." —*Publishers Weekly* (starred review)

"The Montalbano mysteries offer *cose dolci* to the world-lit lover hankering for a whodunit." —*The Village Voice*

Also by Andrea Camilleri

The Shape of Water

The Terra-Cotta Dog

The Snack Thief

Voice of the Violin

Excursion to Tindari

The Smell of the Night

Rounding the Mark

The Patience of the Spider

The Paper Moon

August Heat

The Wings of the Sphinx

The Track of Sand

The Potter's Field

The Age of Doubt

The Dance of the Seagull

To request Penguin Readers Guides by mail
(while supplies last), please call (800) 778-6425
or e-mail reading@us.penguin.com.
To access Penguin Readers Guides online,
visit our Web site at www.penguin.com.

PENGUIN BOOKS

Elvira Giorgianni

TREASURE HUNT

Andrea Camilleri, a bestseller in Italy and Germany, is the author of the popular and *New York Times* bestselling Inspector Montalbano series, as well as historical novels set in nineteenth-century Sicily. The Montalbano series has been translated into thirty-two languages and was adapted for Italian television. *The Potter's Field*, the thirteenth book in the series, was awarded the Crime Writers' Association's International Dagger for the best crime novel translated into English. He lives in Italy.

Stephen Sartarelli is an award-winning translator and the author of three books of poetry.

TREASURE HUNT

ANDREA CAMILLERI

Translated by Stephen Sartarelli

PENGUIN BOOKS

PENGUIN BOOKS
Published by the Penguin Group
Penguin Group (USA) Inc., 375 Hudson Street,
New York, New York 10014, USA

USA | Canada | UK | Ireland | Australia
New Zealand | India | South Africa | China
Penguin Books Ltd, Registered Offices: 80 Strand, London WC2R 0RL, England
For more information about the Penguin Group visit penguin.com

First published in Penguin Books 2013

Originally published in Italian as *La caccia al tesoro* by Sellerio Editore, Palermo.

LIBRARY OF CONGRESS CATALOGING-IN-PUBLICATION DATA
Camilleri, Andrea.
[Caccia al tesoro. English]
Treasure hunt / Andrea Camilleri ; Translated by Stephen Sartarelli.
pages cm—(A Penguin mystery)
"Originally published in Italian as *La caccia al tesoro* by Sellerio Editore, Palermo."
ISBN 978-0-14-312262-3
I. Sartarelli, Stephen, 1954—translator.   II. Title.
PQ4863.A3894C33313 2013
853'.914—dc23   2013016834

Printed in the United States of America
1   3   5   7   9   10   8   6   4   2

Set in Bembo Std
Designed by Jaye Zimet

ALWAYS LEARNING   PEARSON

TREASURE HUNT

That Gregorio Palmisano and his sister Caterina had been churchy people since childhood was known all over town. They never missed a single morning or evening service, not a single Holy Mass or evening's Vespers, and sometimes they even went to church for no reason other than the fact that they felt like it. For the Palmisanos, the faint scent of incense and candle wax lingering in the air after the Mass was better than the smell of ragù to a man who hadn't eaten for ten days.

Always kneeling in the first pew, they didn't bow their heads when praying, but held them high, eyes open wide. But they weren't looking at the great crucifix over the main altar or the Blessed Virgin in sorrow at its feet. No, they never once, not even for a second, took their eyes off the priest, and they watched his every move: the way he turned the pages of the Gospel, the way he gave his benediction, the way he raised his arms when he said *Dominus vobiscum* and then concluded with *Ite, missa est*.

The truth of the matter was that they would have both liked to be priests themselves, to wear surplices, stoles, and vestments, to open the little door of the tabernacle, hold the silver chalice in their hands, administer Holy Communion to the faithful. Both of them, Caterina, too.

In fact when, as a little girl, she told her mother, Matilde, what she wanted to do when she grew up, her mamma firmly corrected her:

"You mean a nun," she said.

"No, Mamma, a priest."

"What? And why do you want to be a priest but not a nun?" Signura Matilde asked with a laugh.

"Because the priest gets to say Mass, and the nuns don't."

In the end they were both forced to work for their father, who was a wholesaler of foodstuffs, which he kept crammed in three large warehouses, one right next to the other.

After their parents died, Gregorio and Caterina changed merchandise, and instead of pasta, cans of tomato preserves, and salted stockfish, they started selling antiques. It was Gregorio's job to go around to the oldest churches in the neighboring towns and the half-dilapidated *palazzi* of nobles once rich and now starving. One of their three warehouses was chock-full of crucifixes, ranging from the kind you hang from your neck on a chain to the life-size variety. There were even three or four naked crosses, huge, heavy replicas of the original, designed for being carried on the shoulder of a penitent during Holy Week processions, as Roman centurions scourged him.

When he turned seventy (she was sixty-eight at the time), they sold the three warehouses, but they'd taken a certain quantity of objects one night to their home on the top floor of a building next to city hall. It was a big apartment with six spacious rooms and a terrace, which the two never used, too big for a brother and sister who had never wanted to marry and who didn't even have any nephews or nieces.

Their religious obsession increased with the reality of no longer having anything to do. They went out only to go to church, always side by side, walking fast, heads down, never returning greetings, only to race back home afterwards and lock themselves in, shutters always closed, as if they were eternally in mourning.

The grocery shopping was done by a woman who used to clean the warehouses for them, but they never allowed her into their apartment. In the morning the woman would find a small piece of paper tacked to the door, on which Caterina had written everything she needed, and the money necessary under the doormat.

When she returned, she would set the shopping bags down on the floor, knock on the door, and call out, before leaving:

"The groceries!"

They didn't own a television, and when they were still antiques dealers, nobody had ever seen them reading a book or a newspaper, but only the breviary, the way priests do.

After about ten years of this, something changed. The Palmisanos stopped going outside, stopped going to church, and never looked out from their balcony, not even when the procession of the town's patron saint went by.

Their only contact, oral or written, with the outside world was with the woman who did the shopping for them.

One morning the people of Vigàta noticed that between the first and second balconies of the Palmisanos' flat, they had hung a large white banner with the words, written in large block letters:

SINNERS, REPENT!

A week later, between the second and third balconies, another banner appeared:

SINNERS, WE WILL PUNISH YOU!

The following week a third one materialized, but this time it covered the entire terrace balustrade and was the largest of all:

WE WILL MAKE YOU PAY FOR YOUR
SINS WITH YOUR LIFE!!!

Once he saw the third banner, Montalbano got worried.

"Don't make me laugh!" Mimì Augello said to him. "They're a couple of senile old dotards who happen to be religious fanatics!"

"Bah!"

"What makes you so concerned?"

"The exclamation points. There are suddenly three, where before there was one."

"So?"

"It may be a sign that they're giving the sinners a deadline, and this is the last warning."

"But who would these sinners happen to be?"

"We're all sinners, Mimì. Have you forgotten? Do you know whether Gregorio Palmisano has a firearms license?"

"I'll go and check."

He returned almost immediately, slightly frowning.

"Yes, he's got a license all right. He requested it when he was dealing antiques and it was granted. A revolver. But he also declared two hunting rifles and a pistol that used to belong to his father."

"Listen, tomorrow I want you to ask Fazio what church they used to go to, and then go and talk to the parish priest."

"But the guy's sworn to the secrecy of the confessional!"

"And you're not going to ask him to reveal any secrets; you only need to find out just how far gone he thinks they are, and whether he thinks their madness is dangerous or not. In the meantime I'll phone the mayor."

"What for?"

"I want him to send a municipal cop to the Palmisanos' place to take down those banners."

———

Officer Landolina of the Municipal Police showed up at the Palmisano home at seven in the evening. Since the Palermo soccer match was coming on TV right after the evening news, he wanted to take care of things early, go back home, eat, and settle into his armchair.

He knocked on the door, but nobody answered. Since

Landolina, a stubborn but scrupulous man, didn't want to waste any time, he not only continued knocking as hard as he could, with his clenched fist, but also started kicking the door until the voice of an elderly man called out:

"Who is it?"

"Police! Open the door!"

"No."

"Open the door right now!"

"Go away, Officer, if you know what's good for you!"

"Don't you threaten me! Open up!"

Gregorio stopped threatening him and simply fired his revolver once through the door.

The bullet grazed Landolina's head, whereupon he turned tail and ran.

After descending the stairs and going out into the main street, the officer saw people fleeing in every direction amidst cries and laments, curses and prayers. From two separate balconies, Gregorio and Caterina had started firing rifles at passersby below.

Thus began the siege of the Palmisanos' little fortress by the forces of order—that is, by Montalbano, Augello, Fazio, Gallo, and Galluzzo. The crowd of onlookers was large but kept at a distance by municipal cops. After an hour of this, the newspapermen and television crews also showed up.

By ten o'clock that evening, seeing that not even their priest, equipped with a bullhorn, could persuade his two elderly parishioners to surrender, Montalbano came to the conclusion that they would have to storm the tiny strong-hold. He sent Fazio out to determine how they might reach the terrace, whether from the roof or from some neighboring apartment. After an hour of careful reconnaissance, Fazio returned to say that it was hopeless: there was no way to reach the roof from any of the other apartments or to approach the Palmisanos' terrace.

The inspector then rang Catarella from his cell phone.

"Call the Montelusa fire department at once—"

"Izz 'ere a fire, Chief?"

"Let me finish! And tell them to come here at once with a ladder that can reach six stories high."

"So there's a fire onna six floor?"

"There isn't any fire!"

"So why's you want the fire department?" Catarella asked with implacable logic.

Cursing the saints, the inspector hung up, dialed the fire department himself, identified himself, and explained what he wanted.

"Right away?" the switchboard operator asked.

"Of course!"

"The problem is that the two vehicles equipped with ladders are occupied at the moment. They could probably be in Vigàta in about an hour. As for the searchlight, there's no problem. I'll send the crew right away."

Right away meant another hour wasted.

Every so often the Palmisanos would fire a few shots with

their rifles and pistols, just to stay sharp. At last the searchlight arrived, got into position, and cast its beam. The entire façade of the building was bathed in a harsh blue light.

"Thank you, Inspector!" the television cameramen cried out.

It looked exactly as if they were shooting a film.

The ladder, however, didn't arrive until after one o'clock in the morning, and was promptly extended until it touched the balustrade covered by the banner.

"All right, I'm going up," said Montalbano. "Fazio, you come up behind me. And Mimì, you go inside with Gallo and Galluzzo and wait outside their door. While I'm keeping them busy on the terrace, I want you to try to force their door and get inside."

No sooner had the inspector set his foot down on the first rung than Gregorio suddenly appeared from behind the banner and fired his pistol. And then disappeared. Montalbano ran for cover in a building entrance and said to Fazio:

"I think it's better if I go up alone. You stay behind on the ground and start firing to give me some cover."

As soon as Fazio fired his first shot, tearing a hole in the banner, the inspector climbed the first rung. He was gripping the ladder with only his left hand, since he had his revolver in his right.

He continued climbing cautiously. He'd reached the height of the fifth floor when suddenly, despite Fazio's gunfire, Gregorio Palmisano reappeared and fired a shot from his revolver that barely missed the inspector.

Montalbano instinctively ducked his head between his shoulders, and in so doing he caught sight of the street below. All at once a cold sweat drenched him from head to toe and he began to feel so dizzy he was in danger of falling. A surge of vomit rose up from the pit of his stomach. He realized that he was in the throes of vertigo, something he'd never experienced before. And now, no doubt with the onset of old age, it suddenly appeared at the worst possible moment.

He held still for a long minute, unable to move, eyes shut tight. But then he clenched his teeth and resumed his climb, even more slowly than before.

When he reached the balustrade, he bolted upright, ready to start firing, but a quick glance revealed that the terrace was deserted. Gregorio had gone back inside, closing the French door behind him, and must certainly be right behind the shutter with his pistol cocked.

"Turn off the spotlight!" Montalbano yelled.

And he leapt onto the terrace, immediately lying down flat on the ground. Gregorio's gunshot arrived on schedule, but the harsh light that had suddenly gone out had left him dazzled, forcing him to fire blindly. Montalbano fired back in turn, but couldn't see anything. Then little by little his eyes returned to normal.

But standing up and running towards the French door while shooting was out of the question, since this time Gregorio was certain to hit him.

As he was wondering what to do, Fazio jumped over the balustrade and lay down beside him.

Now they heard rifle shots coming from inside.

"That's Caterina firing at our men from behind the door," Fazio said in a soft voice.

The terrace was completely bare except for a vase of flowers and a clothesline with things hanging from it; as for anything behind which they might take cover, nothing. Leaning against a wall, however, were three or four long iron poles, possibly the remains of an old gazebo.

"What should we do?" asked Fazio.

"Run over there and grab one of those metal poles. If it's not rusted through, I think you should be able to bust open the French door. Give me your gun. Ready? Here we go . . . One, two, three!"

They stood up, and Montalbano started shooting both pistols, feeling slightly ridiculous, like some sheriff in a 'Murcan movie. Then he pulled up alongside Fazio, who was using the pole as a lever, still shooting, this time at the shutter. At last the French door flew open, and they found themselves in near total darkness, because the large room they had entered was barely illuminated by the faint light of an oil lamp on a small table. It had been some time since the Palmisanos stopped using electrical lighting, and no doubt they no longer had power.

Where was the crazy old man hiding? They heard two rifle shots ring out in a nearby room. It was Caterina fighting off the efforts of Mimì, Gallo, and Galluzzo to break down the front door.

"Go and grab her from behind," Montalbano said to

Fazio, giving him back his gun. "I'll go and look for Gregorio."

Fazio disappeared behind a door that gave onto a hallway.

But there was another door off the room, and it was closed. Montalbano felt certain, for no particular reason, that the old man was behind it. Tiptoeing up to it, he turned the knob, and the door opened slightly. The expected gunshot never came.

And so he flung the door wide open while jumping aside. There was no reaction.

And what was Fazio up to? Why was the old lady still firing away?

He took a deep breath and went in, bent completely over, ready to shoot. And immediately he no longer knew where he was.

It was a large room, densely thicketed with a sort of forest, but of what?

Then he realized what it was and felt paralyzed by an irrational fear.

By the light of another oil lamp he saw dozens and dozens of crucifixes of varying size, ranging from three feet to ceiling-high, all held upright by wooden bases and forming indeed a tangled forest, arranged in such a way that many faced one another, with the arm of one cross cutting slantwise across the arm of the cross beside it, while other, shorter crosses had their backs to the larger crosses but stood face to face with still other crosses of the same height, and so on.

Montalbano became immediately convinced that Gregorio was not in that room and certainly would never start firing and risk striking one or more of the crucifixes. All the same, he couldn't move, being frozen in fear like a child who finds himself alone in an empty church illuminated only by candlelight. At the far end of the large room was an open door, with the dim light of yet another oil lamp filtering through. The inspector eyed that door but was unable to take a single step.

What finally forced him to take the plunge into the woods was a shout from Fazio amidst a horrible mouselike squeaking, which was actually the sound of Caterina's desperate cries.

"Chief! I've got her!"

Montalbano leapt forward, zigzagging between the crucifixes, crashing into one that lurched but did not fall, and then dashed through the far door. He found himself in a room with a double bed.

Gregorio pointed his revolver at him and fired as the inspector dived to the floor. He heard the firing pin go *click*; the gun was empty. He stood up. The old man, who was tall and looked like a skeleton with shoulder-length white hair, was completely naked and staring in disbelief at the revolver still in his hand. With a swift kick, Montalbano sent the gun flying across the room.

Gregorio started crying.

Then the inspector noticed, as a sense of horror very nearly overwhelmed him, that on one of the pillows lay the head of a woman with long blond hair, the rest of her body covered by a sheet. He realized at once that the body was lifeless.

Approaching the bed for a better look, he heard Gregorio order him, in a voice that sounded like sandpaper:

"Don't you dare go near the bride that God sent me!"

He lifted the sheet.

It was a decrepit inflatable doll that had lost some of its hair, was missing an eye, had one deflated tit and little circles and rectangles of gray rubber scattered all over its body. Apparently whenever the doll sprang a leak from old age, Gregorio vulcanized it.

"Salvo, where are you?"

It was Augello.

"I'm over here. Everything's under control."

He heard a strange noise and looked into the neighboring room. Gallo and Galluzzo, equipped with strong battery-powered flashlights, were moving crucifixes in order to create a passageway. When they had finished, Montalbano saw Mimì and Fazio coming forward, flanked by two rows of crucifixes, restraining between them a struggling Caterina Palmisano, who continued to make mousey squeaking noises.

Caterina looked as if she had just stepped out of a horror novel. She was quite short and wearing a filthy nightgown riddled with holes, had disheveled, yellowish-white hair and big, bugged-out eyes, and only one long, blood-curdling tooth in her drooling mouth.

"I curse you!" Caterina said, looking at Montalbano with wild eyes. "You shall burn alive in the fires of Hell!"

"We can talk about that later," the inspector replied.

"I'd call an ambulance," Mimì suggested. "And have them both sent to the insane asylum or whatever it's called these days."

"We certainly can't keep them in a holding cell," Fazio added.

"All right, call an ambulance and take them outside. Thank the firemen and send them home. Did they break the door down?"

"No, there was no need. I opened it from the inside," said Fazio.

"And what are you gonna do?" Augello asked.

"Did she have both of the rifles with her?" he asked Fazio instead of answering.

"Yessir."

"Then there must be another gun around the house, the father's pistol. I'm going to have a look around. You two go now, but leave me one of those flashlights."

Left alone, Montalbano stuck his gun in his pocket and took a step.

But then he thought better of it and took the gun back out. True, there wasn't anyone around anymore, but it was the place itself that made him uneasy. The flashlight cast gigantic shadows of the crucifixes on the walls. Montalbano raced through the passageway created by his men and found himself in the room that gave onto the terrace.

Feeling the need for a little fresh air, he went outside. And although the downtown air stank of the smoke of the cement factory and automobile exhausts, it smelled to him like fine mountain air compared to what he'd been breathing inside the Palmisanos' apartment.

He went back inside and headed for the door that led to the hallway. Immediately on the left were three rooms in a row, while the wall on the right was solid.

The first room was Caterina's bedroom. Atop the chest of drawers, the bedside table, and the bookcase, hundreds of little statuettes of the Madonna had been amassed, each with a little light on it in front. On the walls were another hundred or so holy pictures, all of the Blessed Virgin. Each picture had a little wooden shelf under it, on which shone a little light. It looked like a cemetery at night.

The door to the second room was locked, but the key was in the keyhole. The inspector turned it, opened the door, and went inside. By the beam of the flashlight he saw that it was an enormous room crammed full of pianos, three of them grand pianos, one with the fallboard open. Enormous spiderwebs twinkled between the different pianos. Then all at once the grand piano began to play. As Montalbano shouted in fear and withdrew, he heard the entire musical scale resonate, *do re mi fa sol la ti.* Were there living dead in that accursed apartment? Ghosts? He was bathed in sweat, the gun in his hand trembling slightly, but nevertheless found the strength to raise his arm and illuminate the great room with his flashlight. And he finally saw the ghostly musician.

It was a large rat running wildly from one piano to another. Apparently it had run across the open keyboard.

The third room off the hallway was the kitchen. But it smelled so bad that the inspector didn't have the courage to go in. He would have one of his men come and look for the pistol tomorrow.

When he went back down into the street, everybody was gone. He headed for his car, which was parked near the town hall, started it up, and headed home to Marinella.

At home he took a long shower, but did not go to bed afterwards. Instead he went and sat down on the veranda.

And so, instead of being awakened by the first light of day as was usually the case, it was he who watched the day awaken.

2

He decided not to go and lie down in bed. Two or three hours of sleep wouldn't have done him any good. On the contrary, it would simply have left him feeling woozier than ever.

Actually—he thought as he went into the kitchen to prepare another four-cup espresso pot—what had happened to him the previous night was just like a nightmare that resurfaces in the mind all at once the moment you wake up and remains in the memory, though gradually fading, for only a day, so that, after another night's sleep, the nightmare vanishes, and you have trouble remembering it, as the contours and details blur little by little until it becomes like a mosaic besieged by time, with large patches of gray wall where the colored tesserae have fallen off.

Therefore, he needed only be patient another twenty-four hours and then he could forget what he saw in the Palmisanos' apartment and what happened to him there.

Because he simply couldn't shake off the fright the place had given him.

The forest of crucifixes, the inflatable doll that had grown old with its owner, the great room full of pianos and

17

spiderwebs, the musical rat, the flickering light of the oil lamps . . . And Gregorio Palmisano, naked and skinny as a skeleton, and Caterina with only one tooth . . . For a horror film, it wasn't a bad beginning.

The problem, however, was that it wasn't a fiction, but a reality, though a reality so absurd as to be very nearly a fiction.

But the real problem, which he tried to hide with all this talk of nightmares, truth, and fiction, actually concerned something he didn't want to face up to—that is, the difference between his behavior and that of his men.

Nor did he face up to it now, since the coffee was ready, and he took advantage of it.

Carrying it out onto the veranda, he drank the first cup of his second pot.

He gazed for a long time at the sky, the sea, the beach. The dawning day had to be relished little by little, like a jam too sweet.

"Good morning, Inspector," the usual solitary fisherman greeted him, busy with his boat.

Montalbano raised a hand in reply.

"Happy fishing!" he said.

"Could I say something?" asked Montalbano Two, suddenly appearing and launching into his commentary without waiting for an answer. *"The problem that you're doing your utmost to avoid can be boiled down to two questions. The first is: Why were Gallo and Galluzzo not the least bit frightened by the forest of crucifixes and in fact seemed rather indifferent as they moved them*

aside? The second: Why, when he saw the inflatable doll, was Mimì not taken aback, but merely smiled at the thought that Gregorio Palmisano was a horny old goat?"

"Well, everyone is different and behaves accordingly," said Montalbano One, caught off-guard . . .

"That's trite but true, but the problem is that there was a time in the life of our inspector when he would have reacted the same way as Gallo and Galluzzo in front of those crucifixes, and like Mimì in front of the doll. At one time in his life."

"Would you guys knock it off?" said Montalbano, realizing where Number Two was headed.

"I would like to make my point. In my opinion, the good inspector has changed since then, and it's because of his age. But he has a lot of trouble admitting it, indeed he refuses to admit it. For example, he acts as if he's had an eye transplant."

"What the hell are you talking about?"

"I realize they don't exist yet—eye transplants, that is. But old age has done it for him, performed the operation. He's now got two new eyes grafted onto an aging head."

"What do you mean, *new* eyes?"

"Much more sensitive. Not only do you see the things in front of you, you also perceive the aura around those things. It's like a light, watery vapor that rises from them and—"

"And in your opinion, what kind of 'aura' was there around the inflatable doll?" Montalbano One asked defiantly.

"An aura of despair and solitude. That of a lonely man who spent his nights in the arms of a lifeless doll instead of a living being, and who probably calls it 'My love.'"

"Get to the point."

"The point is that the inspector is losing his cool, his sense of detachment, in the face of things. He's letting himself be involved and troubled by them. And though before, too, he would let himself be taken in, now, with the years, he's become too . . . well, too vulnerable."

"That's enough of that," said Montalbano, suddenly getting up. "You guys are starting to piss me off."

Contrary to what he'd decided, he went to bed to get a couple of hours' sleep, and when the alarm clock went off, he woke up, feeling totally bleary, as expected.

A shower, shave, and clean underwear freshened him as best they could, at any rate putting him in a condition to show his face at the office.

Seeing him come in, Catarella leapt to his feet and started clapping.

"Bravo, Chief! Bravo!"

"What the hell's wrong with you? Are we at the theater or something?"

"Ahh, Chief, Chief! Good God were you good! Man, so nimmel, so fast! Like a agrobat on a trappist!"

"Who?"

"You, Chief! It was better 'n a movie! An' 'ey showed it onna TV 'iss mornin'."

"*I* was on TV?!"

"Yessir, Chief, you was! When you's climin' the firemin's ladder, gun in yer 'and, y'know who y'look jess like?"

"No."

"Jess like Brussi Vìllisi, y'know, the 'Murcan actor who's always in shoot-ats an' boinin' bildinz an' sinkin' ships . . ."

"All right, all right, settle down and get Fazio for me."

All he needed was a ball-ache like this! Now the half of town that hadn't seen him live in action last night could catch the replay on TV! Bruce Willis! Right! It was more like a Marx Brothers routine!

"Good morning, Chief."

"How'd things end up with the Palmisanos?"

"How do you expect? Prosecutor Tallarita threw the book at 'em. Resisting arrest, attempted multiple homicide, attempted massacre . . ."

"Where'd they take them?"

"To a clinic for the mentally ill, on twenty-four-hour watch."

"That seems a bit excessive. They haven't got any weapons, so what are they gonna—"

"Do you know what Caterina did to an orderly there, Chief?"

"No. What'd she do?"

"She broke a chair over his head!"

"Why'd she do that?"

"Because the guy was clearly an Arab, and so for her, he was an enemy of God."

"Listen, I want to send somebody to look for a pistol that must be hidden away somewhere in the Palmisanos' apartment."

"I'll take care of it right away. I'll send Galluzzo and a couple of other guys."

Half an hour later, Fazio knocked on the door and came in.

"I'm sorry, Chief, but yesterday, when you left the Palmisanos' apartment, did you close the door? I left the keys in the keyhole after opening the door for Inspector Augello."

Montalbano thought about this for a few seconds.

"You know I don't even remember whether I closed it or not? Why do you ask?"

"Because Galluzzo called me just now and said he found the door to the apartment wide open."

"Was anything missing?"

"According to Galluzzo, probably nothing's missing. It's all more or less the way he remembered leaving it last night. But how can you really tell in all that clutter?"

I congratulate you, dear Inspector, for the consummate bravery, the sublime disregard for danger you displayed when left alone in that famous house of horrors. Your long struggle with the musical rat wore you out so completely that you ran away at full speed, actually forgetting to close the door. Not bad. Congratulations again.

"Tell me something, Fazio, I'm curious."

"Sure, Chief."

"Did you get a strange feeling from that apartment?"

"Don't remind me, Chief! When I saw that enormous room packed full of crucifixes, pardon my language, but I nearly shat my pants!"

He would have liked to stand up and hug Fazio. So they were all creeped out and afraid. Except they hadn't let on. And so his morning cogitations had been for naught.

At one o'clock he went to Enzo's to eat. He was extremely hungry, being behind in his eating, having had no time for supper the previous evening amidst all the pandemonium. He sat down at his usual table.

The TV was on and tuned in to TeleVigàta. The sound was turned down so softly that he almost couldn't hear, but the images he was seeing were of the inside of the Palmisanos' apartment.

Some asshole journalist must have taken advantage of the door he'd left open, going inside and filming the home of the crazy old pair of loons. Apparently the guy had used some sort of battery-powered lamp for lighting, which, in casting its beam edgewise onto the crucifixes and pianos, showed them emerging from the darkness with a sinister, menacing air, exactly the way they had looked to Montalbano the night before.

"Hello, Inspector, what can I get for you?"

"Come back in five minutes."

Now the cameraman was in Gregorio's bedroom. And he lingered for at least five minutes on the inflatable doll, first showing a full-length shot, then a close-up of the hairless spots on the head, the missing eye, the shrivelled breast, then one by one the patches that Gregorio had made to keep it from deflating, which looked like so many little wounds covered by adhesive bandages.

"So, what can I get for you?"

How was it that he suddenly no longer felt hungry?

He ate so little that he didn't even feel the need to take his customary meditative stroll. And so he went back to the office and started signing papers. Nothing of any substance had happened for a good month. Of course the Palmisano incident had certainly provided a little excitement, even a touch of tragicomedy, but it hadn't had any major consequences, and there hadn't been any dead or wounded. On several occasions during the past month, he had, in fact, thought of taking a few days off and going to Boccadasse to be with Livia. But he'd always let it slide, afraid that some unforeseen development might force him to interrupt his vacation. And who would deal with Livia then?

"Galluzzo finally found the pistol," said Fazio, coming in.

"Where was it?"

"In Caterina's room. Hidden inside a hollow statue of the Madonna."

"Any new developments?"

"Dead calm. Did you know that Catarella has a theory about it?"

"About what?"

"About the fact that there are less robberies."

"And how does he explain it?"

"He says that the robbers, the local ones, who rob the homes of working poor or snatch women's purses, are ashamed."

"Of what?"

"Of their big-time colleagues. The CEOs who drive their companies to bankruptcy after making off with people's savings, the banks who are always finding a way to screw their customers, the big companies that steal public funds. Whereas they, the petty thieves who have to make do with ten euros or a broken TV or a computer that doesn't work . . . they feel ashamed, and don't feel like stealing anymore."

As could have been expected, at midnight, TeleVigàta broadcast a special report covering the entire Palmisano incident.

Naturally they showed footage of Montalbano climbing the ladder while Gregorio was shooting at him from the terrace, and the whole thing, seen from the outside, confirmed Catarella's interpretation. That is, it really did look as though nothing could stop the inspector. You needed only to see the determination with which he climbed over the balustrade with a gun in one hand and hear the authority with which he ordered the people on the ground to turn off the search-light.

In short, a moment worthy of the TV series *Captains Courageous.*

None of the fear, trembling, or vertigo he had felt half-way up showed in the video. Luckily there was no device in the world, not even an X-ray machine, not even a CAT scanner, that could show inner distress and well-concealed fear. But when the footage of the inflatable doll began, Montalbano turned off the TV.

He just couldn't stand it. It made him feel weirder than if it was actually a real, live girl in flesh and blood.

Before going to bed, he phoned Livia.

"I saw you, you know," she said right off the bat.

"Where?"

"On TV, on the national news."

Fucking bastards. The TeleVigàta crew had sold their story!

"I was really scared for you," Livia continued.

"When?"

"When you had that moment of vertigo on the ladder."

"You're right. But nobody seemed to notice."

"I did. But couldn't you have sent Augello up there instead? He's so much younger than you. You really can't be doing these kinds of things anymore at your age!"

Montalbano started to worry. So now Livia, too, was starting in with this crap about his age?

"You talk as if I was fucking Methuselah, for Chrissakes!"

"Don't use obscenities, I won't stand for it! Who ever mentioned Methuselah? You're becoming so neurotic!"

With a start like that, the whole thing could only end on a sour note.

———

"Ahh Chief, Chief! Ahh Chief! Hizzoner the C'mishner's been callin' f'yiz since eight aclack! Jeezis, was he mad! 'E sez 'e wants yiz a call 'im emergently straightaways!"

"All right, give him a ring and pass the call to me," said Montalbano, heading for his office.

His conscience was clean. Since nothing had happened of late, he hadn't had the opportunity to do anything that might appear a sin of commission or omission in the eyes of the commissioner.

"Montalbano?"

"Yes, sir, what can I do for you?"

"Would you please explain to me why you allowed several television cameramen to do whatever the hell they pleased in the home of those two crazy old people?"

"But I never—"

"Just know that I've been bombarded with telephone calls of protest—from the bishop's office to the Union of Catholic Fathers, to the FaFa Club to the—"

"I'm sorry sir, I didn't quite get the name of that club."

"FaFa. Would you prefer FF? The full name is the Faith and Family Club."

"But what are they protesting?"

"They're offended by the images of that obscene inflat-able doll."

"Ah, I see. At any rate, I didn't allow anyone to go in there."

"Oh, no? Then how did they get in?"

"Through the door, I would imagine."

"Breaking the seals?"

The place had never been sealed off. Should he have ordered it sealed? At any rate, seals or no seals, he should at least have closed the door.

His only hope was to start talking legalese-bureaucra-tese, the kind where after a couple of sentences nobody understands a fucking thing anymore.

"Mr. Commissioner, if I may. In the case in point, we hadn't ascertained any conditions whereby we should have recourse to the application of said seals, given that while the apartment in question had been the scene of behavior qualifi-able, at the very least, as violent, we were not cognizant of any harm having come to anyone's person as a result of said be-havior, and therefore—"

"Fine, fine, but in entering without authorization, they committed a serious infraction."

"A very serious infraction. And there may be more," said the inspector, trying to up the ante.

"What do you mean?"

Pile on the legalese-bureaucratese.

"Who's to say the cameraman and journalist didn't take

some of the objects found on the premises? With its volumi-
nous spatial capacity, that apartment could be termed more
than a civilian residence. It may well be classifiable as an
antiques warehouse, in view of the fact that it contains, however uninventoried, a wealth of artistically sculpted gold
crosses, illustrated Bibles of untold value, rosaries of mother-
of-pearl, silver, and gold, as well as—"

"Fine, fine, I'm going to take the necessary measures,"
the commissioner interrupted him, put off by Montalbano's
tone of voice.

And thus the folks at TeleVigàta, having a few cats to
comb, would learn their lesson.

On the midday news broadcast, TeleVigàta's purse-lipped
prince of opinion, Pippo Ragonese, the one with a face like
a chicken's ass, said angrily that the broadcasting station,
"known for its absolute independence of judgment," had
been subjected to "strong pressure from a variety of sources"
in an attempt to halt any further broadcasting of the news
feature on the Palmisano home, particularly the footage involving the doll. He let it be known that the journalist and
cameraman who had entered the apartment were in danger
of being indicted for "breaking and entering and theft of art
objects."

In the face of such intimidation, Ragonese solemnly proclaimed that as of that moment, and for the entire afternoon

and evening until the eight P.M. news edition, TeleVigàta would broadcast nothing but the images of the inflatable doll.

And so they did.

But only until six P.M., because at that time two carabinieri showed up and confiscated the videotape by order of the prefect.

By the following morning, needless to say, all the national papers and television news programs were talking about the affair. A few were against the confiscation; one of the most important national dailies, the one printed in Rome, published the headline:

Is There No Limit to the Ridiculousness?

Others instead were in favor. In fact, the other major newspaper, the one printed in Milan, ran the headline:

The Death of Good Taste

And there wasn't a single stand-up comic on television that evening who didn't appear onstage with an inflatable doll.

That night, Montalbano had a dream which, if it wasn't about an actual inflatable doll, as would have been logical and predictable, was about something that came very close.

He was making love to a beautiful young blonde who worked as a salesgirl in a mannequin factory that was deserted, as it was past closing time. They were lying on a sofa in the sales office, surrounded by at least ten mannequins, male and female, who stared fixedly at them, polite little smiles on their lips.

"C'mon, c'mon," the girl kept saying to him, her eyes on a large clock on the wall, because they both knew what the problem was. She had obtained permission to become human, but if they didn't manage to bring their business to a happy conclusion, she would turn back into a mannequin forever.

"C'mon, c'mon . . ."

They finally succeeded, with only three seconds left on the clock. The mannequins in the room applauded.

He woke up and ran into the bathroom to take a shower. But how could it be that at fifty-seven he was still having the dreams of a twenty-year-old? Maybe old age wasn't quite so near at hand as it seemed? The dream reassured him.

━━━━━

As he was driving to work, his car's motor made a strange noise and then suddenly stalled, eliciting a deafening chorus of screeching tires, horn blasts, curses, and insults. He managed to start it up again after a brief spell, but he decided the time had come to take the car to the mechanic's. There were many and sundry things that either didn't work or had a mind of their own.

3

The mechanic had a look at the engine, brakes, and electrical system and shook his head in dismay. Exactly like a doctor beside the bed of a terminally ill patient.

"I'm afraid she's ready to be junked, Inspector."

The use of that verb set his nerves on edge. Whenever he heard it, whenever he read it, his cojones immediately started to go into a spin. And it wasn't the only word that had this effect on him. There were others: securitize, contingency, restructuring, as per, precurrent, and dozens more.

Languages long dead invented wonderful words they handed down to us for eternity.

Whereas our modern languages, when they died— which was inevitable, since every tongue on earth was becoming a colony of American English, itself dying a slow death by suicide—what words would they hand down to posterity? Junked? Scam? Keisters? Kickback? Normalcy?

"That's the furthest thing from my mind," Montalbano snapped rudely.

Another day of dead calm, as Fazio called it, went by at the station. That evening the inspector had Gallo drive him home. It would be another three days before he got his car back.

After eating the mullet in broth and the caponata Adelina had made for him, he continued sitting outside on the veranda.

He felt torn. He would have liked to leave for Boccadasse the very next day, but perhaps should have done so earlier. Too much time had gone by with nothing happening, and therefore the probability that nothing would continue to happen had lessened greatly.

After smoking two cigarettes, he felt like getting into bed and starting that novel by Simenon, *The President*, which he had bought after going to the garage.

He went inside and locked the French door to the veranda. Picking up the book, which he had left on the table, he realized he'd left the light on in the entrance hall. As he went to turn it off, he noticed a white envelope on the floor, which someone had apparently slipped under the door. A perfectly normal-looking letter envelope.

Was it there when he'd come in and he simply hadn't noticed it? Or had someone put it there while he was out on the veranda?

Written in block letters on the envelope were the words: FOR SALVO MONTALBANO. And, on the upper left: *Treasure Hunt*. He opened it. A half-sheet of paper with a sort of poem:

Three times three
is not thirty-three

*and six times six
is not sixty-six.*

*The figure thus obtained
another number shall ordain.
Add your age to the raffle
and the riddle unravel.*

What was this bullshit? Some kind of joke? And why hadn't they sent it through the mail?

The last thing he felt like doing was solving riddles or playing treasure hunt at one o'clock in the morning.

He slipped the envelope and letter into the pocket of the jacket he normally kept in the entrance and went to bed, bringing the book along.

It was almost nine by the time he got to the office. He'd turned the light out rather late the night before, unable to put the book down. Some ten minutes later Catarella rang him.

"Ah, Chief, Chief! Onna line 'ere's a woman witta womanly voice raisin' 'er voice so I dunno what 'er voice is raisin' cuz she's raisin' 'er voice!"

"Did she ask for me?"

"I dunno, Chief."

He really didn't feel like having his ears ringing with the voice of a woman who raised her voice when she raised her voice.

"Pass the call to Inspector Augello."

Less than three minutes later, Mimì came in, looking dead serious and rather upset.

"There's a totally hysterical woman who says that when she went to take her garbage out, she saw a corpse in the trash bin."

"Did she say what street it was on?"

"Via Brancati 18."

"Okay. Grab somebody and go there."

Mimì hesitated.

"Actually I'd told Beba I would take her and Salvuccio this morning to . . ."

Another irritation. Of course he'd been pleased when Mimì and his wife Beba had decided to name their son after him. But he really couldn't stand to hear him called Salvuccio.

"I get the picture. I'll go to Via Brancati myself. But I want you to call Forensics, the prosecutor, and Pasquano right away."

Gallo simply couldn't find this goddamned Via Brancati.

They'd been going round and round fruitlessly for the past half hour, and of all the people they asked, not one appeared to have ever heard of the street.

"Let's go and ask at city hall," Fazio suggested.

But Gallo'd got it in his thick head that he wanted to find it himself. And there was nothing worse than an agitated Gallo at the wheel. Sure enough he turned the wrong way onto a one-way street at high speed.

"Be careful!"

"But there's nobody on the street!"

And at that exact moment a car that had just turned the corner appeared suddenly before them.

Montalbano closed his eyes. It was a narrow street, and Gallo swerved wildly away, crashing into the outdoor stall of a fruit and vegetables shop. Tomatoes, oranges, lemons, grapes, chicory, potatoes, escarole, eggplant, and the rest went flying, turning to mush on the street and sidewalk.

The shop owner came out in a rage and started making a scene. The whole thing risked wasting several hours of their time, but Montalbano quickly showed the man his papers and told him to send the bill to the police station. The man agreed at once to do so, obviously seeing a chance to claim triple the damages.

They resumed going round and round to no end.

All at once the inspector remembered the criteria that every zoning office, in every town hall in Italy—all of them, without exception, from the big cities to the smallest towns—used for naming their streets. The most central streets were without fail always named after abstract things, like liberty, republic, and independence; the slightly less central streets, after political figures of the past, like Cavour, Zanardelli, Crispi, and others; the streets just outside of those, after other, more recent political figures, like De Gasperi, Einaudi, and Togliatti. And then, as you got farther and farther from the center, came heroes, military leaders, mathematicians, scientists, and industrialists, until you came to a few dentists. Reserved for last, for the streets on the most remote outskirts, the shabbiest ones, those bordering on the open country, were the names of artists, writers, sculptors, poets, painters, and musicians.

And indeed Via Vitaliano Brancati consisted of four little cottages with chickens running free outside. Which, in a sense, was a fortunate thing.

Because standing around a woman of about forty dressed all in black and sitting on a chair and holding a wet handkerchief to her forehead were a woman of about seventy and two men. Whereas on most other streets there would have been a huge mob they would have had to disperse with billy clubs.

In front of one of the cottages was a lone dumpster. The dead body could only be in there.

"Has anyone other than the signora opened it?"

The elderly woman and the two men shook their heads. Fazio lifted the lid and Montalbano stood on tiptoe to look inside.

The only thing in there was the body.

"Holy fucking shit!" said the inspector.

Then, turning to Fazio:

"Hold it steady for me."

He wanted to double-check, so flabbergasted had he been by what he'd seen. Fazio grabbed onto the edge with both hands to act as a counterweight. Montalbano hoisted himself up, holding himself in the air with his hands resting on the rim of the dumpster, then lowered himself halfway inside, bending over with his belly resting on the rim. He touched the body, pulled himself back up, then landed back with both feet on the ground.

Fazio shot him an inquiring glance. The woman who'd been sitting had also stood up and came forward with the other two. Montalbano, however, remained silent, dazed and speechless.

"It's an inflatable doll," he said at last.

How many of them could there be, in Vigàta?

"So much the better," said Fazio. "We can leave it right there."

"No," said Montalbano, "pull it out."

Fazio got Gallo to help, and they laid it down on the ground and just stood there staring at it in silence.

All three policemen turned sullen and grave, because the doll was identical in every way to the one that Gregorio Palmisano had kept in his bed. Some of the hair had fallen out, an eye was missing, one of the tits deflated, and the body was covered with many little round and square rubber patches.

At that exact moment Dr. Pasquano arrived, followed by the ambulance for transporting corpses. Seeing the doctor appear, Montalbano realized he would rather be in a forest at that moment, surrounded by wild animals. And indeed, Pasquano, like the asshole he was, started clowning around.

He squatted down beside the doll and started to examine it.

"The body shows no signs of violence," he said.

"Iss a doll, Doctor," said the woman who'd discovered it. She was still standing there, not quite knowing what to do.

"Take her away," said Pasquano. "I've got work to do." Then he went on:

"She probably died of natural causes."

"That's enough, now, Doctor," said Montalbano.

Pasquano sprang up like a cricket, red in the face.

"So you're not going to ask me the hour of death, eh?" he blurted out. "Can't you see you're no longer able to distinguish between a corpse and a doll? Next time, before inconveniencing me, make sure the dead body's really a body and not a mannequin! Of all the lamebrained crap . . ."

He got back in his car, cursing, and drove off.

The two stretcher bearers came slowly forward, looking doubtful. They cast a glance at the doll, and one of them scratched his head. The other asked:

"Are we supposed to take this away with us?"

"No, no, you can leave too, thanks," said the inspector, feeling annihilated.

Naturally, as soon as Pasquano was gone, Forensics arrived with the entire team, a small van and two cars. Out of the first vehicle stepped Vanni Arquà, chief of Forensics, whom the inspector found truly insufferable. And the feeling was quite mutual.

"Don't unload anything, there's no need," Montalbano

said to the Forensics crew, who were starting to take boxes, trunks, and cameras out of the van.

"Why?" asked Arquà.

"There's been a mistake."

Arquà went and looked at the body, then returned with a dark expression on his face.

"It's just some stupid joke!"

"It's not a joke, Arquà! What happened was that—"

"I'm going to report this at once to the commissioner!"

"Do whatever the fuck you like."

And they left, too.

Then, moments later, the last to arrive, as usual, was Prosecutor Tommaseo, who drove like a drunken dog. He stepped out of the car, seeming short of breath.

"Sorry, sorry, I had a little accident . . ."

Seeing the doll stretched out on the ground, his eyes lit up.

"But it's a woman!" he said, rushing up.

Like a vampire on the wagon. Whenever there was a woman involved, Tommaseo would lose his head. He went crazy for crimes of passion, for pretty girls who met a bad end, for any sort of killing that had anything to do with sex.

"What is the meaning of this?" he asked the inspector in a disappointed tone of voice upon realizing what he was looking at.

"This lady here saw it in the trash bin and thought it was a woman's body. Unfortunately, sir, I wasn't able to alert you in time of the mistake."

"Please excuse me," Tommaseo said to all present. He didn't seem the least bit angry, like the others. Then he took Montalbano by the arm and pulled him aside.

"Listen," he said in a soft voice, "just for my information, do you have any idea where they sell these kinds of dolls?"

Finally, after the others were all gone, they loaded the doll into the trunk and drove back to the station without exchanging a word.

He cleared his desk of the several thousand sheets of paper on it and laid the doll down across it lengthwise.

"I need the other one," he said to Fazio, who was staring at him in silence, unable to comprehend what the inspector had in mind.

"What other one?"

"Palmisano's doll."

Fazio gawked at him, open-mouthed.

"Why, isn't this it?"

"No."

"What! Are you sure?"

"Absolutely. At the most it's a twin."

"How about that! I was thinking that the guys from TeleVigàta had taken it away to get some better shots of it and then, since they couldn't take it back, had thrown it into the dumpster."

"How much you want to bet there are two?"

"How many inflatable dolls can there be around Vigàta?"

"I was wondering the same thing. Now go."

But Fazio didn't move. He seemed doubtful.

"How on earth am I going to get it here?"

"What do you mean?"

"Chief, how am I going to come down the stairs with that thing in my arms? What if some neighbor comes out and sees me?"

"What can I say? You're a policeman in the service of—"

"But I'm embarrassed!"

"Don't make me laugh!"

"Please, just send someone else."

"Tell me the truth, Fazio. This isn't just some kind of excuse, is it? You wouldn't be afraid of going back into that place, would you?"

"Well, yes, a little."

Montalbano understood him well.

"Then send Gallo and Galluzzo. Oh, and listen: I'm pretty sure there's a chest somewhere here at the station. I believe I saw one in the garage. Tell them to bring it along and put the doll in it."

It had been a mistake to lay the doll down on his desk. Now he couldn't write anything, and to answer the phone, he would have to lean on its belly. The whole thing disgusted him a little. On top of everything else, they'd pulled it out of a garbage bin. It was probably best to put her on the floor.

Grabbing the doll by the armpits, he lifted her, stood her up, and at that moment Mimì Augello appeared.

"Ah, excuse me, I can see you're busy, I'll come back later. But take my advice, when you want to do certain things, you should lock the door."

"Come on, Mimì, don't be an idiot, just come in and sit down."

"Why are you so interested in Palmisano's doll?"

"Jesus, what a pain! This isn't Palmisano's doll!"

And he told him the whole story.

"I've sent a couple of our men to get the other one," he said to conclude.

"Why?"

"To compare them. I want to see if they're exactly alike."

"And if they're not, what the hell do you care?"

"Mimì, if you can't figure it out on your own, I can't help you. I'll tell you later."

When Gallo and Galluzzo brought in Palmisano's doll, he had them lay her down on the floor beside the other one.

"Jesus, they're identical!" Gallo exclaimed, looking at them in amazement.

"How can that be?" Galluzzo wondered.

Montalbano had some idea as to how, but since by now it was lunchtime, he said nothing. He wanted to put the papers back on the desk, but became immediately discouraged by how many there were. And so on his way out he asked

Catarella to put his office back in order and to have a magnifying glass waiting for him when he got back.

He ate so disaffectedly that Enzo reproached him.

"You didn't do me justice today, Inspector."

As there was no need to go for a walk along the jetty, he went straight back to his office. Entering the room, he very nearly had a heart attack.

Catarella had put the two dolls in the two armchairs, and they looked as if they were chatting casually.

Cursing, he laid them back down on the floor, about a foot and a half apart. On his desk, which was now covered again with papers, lay a magnifying glass. He grabbed it and knelt down to examine the empty eye socket of Palmisano's doll through the lens. Then he studied the eye socket of the other doll, the one from the dumpster. Next he tore a round rubber patch off the latter's belly, just above the belly button, and then repeated the operation with the other doll.

After he'd been working in this fashion for a spell, he heard Mimì's voice outside the door.

"Discover anything, Holmes?"

"Yes."

"What?"

"Elementary, my dear Watson. I've discovered that you're an asshole," the inspector said, then he got up and sat down behind his desk.

"No, seriously, what were you looking at with the magnifying glass?"

"I was checking whether or not there was a plausible answer to the question I had asked myself."

"Which was?"

"I'll answer you with another question. In your opinion, can two things manufactured at the same time, but then kept rather far apart and used differently over time—let's say two bicycles—can they grow old, lose parts, become punctured in exactly the same way and in the exact same places?"

"I don't understand."

"Let me give you an example. Let's say two women go to the market and buy two identical cooking pots. Thirty years later, we find one of them. It's beaten up, missing the left handle, dented at the base, and has two holes on the bottom, one three millimeters wide, and the other two and a half millimeters. Got that?"

"Got it."

"Then, inside a dumpster we find another identical pot, with the exact same characteristics: the missing left handle, the dent, the two holes, and so on. Does it seem possible to you that the two pots, though used by two different women and likely with different frequency, could deteriorate in exactly the same way?"

"Impossible."

"And yet these two dolls appear to have succeeded at doing just that. And that's my point. Have a good look at them."

"I have, and I can't figure it out."

"Do you know what the only possible explanation is?"

"You tell me."

"With the first doll, Palmisano's doll, the aging process, so to speak, took place naturally, through the wear and tear of use and the passage of time. With the second, the one found in the bin, the damage was created artificially."

"Are you joking?"

"Not in the least. Someone who owned a doll exactly like Palmisano's, but much better preserved, saw the images broadcast by TeleVigàta, recorded them, and used them as a guide to reproduce the exact same damage on his doll."

"How can you possibly know that?"

"You can clearly see that the eye of the dumpster doll was removed with a clean cut, from a blade, whereas on Palmisano's doll the rubber around the missing eye came apart on its own, causing the eyeball to fall out. On top of this, the holes in the dumpster doll were made with an awl, so that if you examine them with a magnifying glass, you can see they're all the same. Whereas on the other doll, each hole is totally different from the others; one is bigger, another one is slightly smaller . . ."

"But why would anyone waste all that time doing something so pointless?"

"Maybe there is a point to it. Actually, there must be a point to it. We just don't know what it is."

4

They went back to studying the dolls. Montalbano then asked:

"Do you know anything about these kinds of dolls?"

"I've never had any need of them," Mimì said, slightly miffed.

"I don't doubt that for even a millisecond. Your prowess as cock of the walk has never been called into question and never will be, I suspect. I simply wanted to know if you could give me a little information."

Augello thought about this for a moment.

"I once saw a documentary on some TV station I pick up with the satellite dish. These two dolls here are antiquated, primitive models, really. Nowadays they make them out of different materials, such as foam rubber, so they're not inflatable anymore, and they look like real women. It's a little spooky."

"So what period would you say these two are from?"

"I dunno, maybe about thirty years ago."

"Tommaseo this morning asked me where they were sold, and I said I had no idea. Do you?"

"Well, over the Internet . . ."

"Forget the Internet. I'm talking about these two. You can tell Tommaseo about the Internet, since it's clear he wants to buy one. But where could you buy these things thirty years ago?"

"Well, they certainly weren't making them in Italy. Bear in mind that before they're inflated they don't take up much space. I'm sure they were mailed from abroad in parcels so that you couldn't tell from the outside what was inside, and they probably wrote something like 'garments' or suchlike on it. And to order them you only had to know the address."

"So therefore, about thirty years ago, two different people in Vigàta—Gregorio Palmisano and some unknown—supposedly ordered, at more or less the same time, two identical dolls."

"So it would seem."

"Then, thirty years later, the unknown man happens to see Palmisano's doll on TV and makes it so that his doll looks in every way like Palmisano's."

"Fine, Salvo, but we keep coming back to the same question: Why did he do it?"

"And why did he get rid of it by throwing it into the dumpster?" the inspector added.

They sat there in silence.

"Listen," Mimì said suddenly, looking him straight in the eye. "You're not becoming a little obsessed, are you?"

"With what?"

"With this business of the dolls. You're not going to start

investigating this the way you did a while back with that horse that was killed?"

"Come on, what do you think this is? I'm just curious, that's all."

But he was lying. There was something about this whole affair that disturbed him.

When it came time to call Gallo for a ride home, it occurred to him that he couldn't very well leave those dolls in his office. Catarella was liable to show someone in when the inspector wasn't there, and one could only imagine what a fine impression that would make! He could have them put in storage, or just throw them away outright.

But something inside told him that they might at some point prove useful.

And so he had them put in the trunk and took them home with him, where he stored them in the closet in which Adelina kept the things she needed for cleaning the house.

He looked at them again, one beside the other, upright. In fact the doll from the dumpster was not identical to its twin.

Now that they were standing, the difference became clearer. The tit on the second doll was flat and wrinkled, yes, but it had three less wrinkles. That detail had been the hardest one to copy, and hadn't come out well.

Perhaps that was why the unknown person had thrown it into the trash bin?

And, if so, did this mean he would try to do better? But where would he ever find a third doll?

In taking the cigarettes and lighter from his jacket pocket, he inadvertently touched an envelope. He took it out and looked at it.

It was the one he'd found under the door the previous evening. He'd forgotten all about it.

The treasure hunt.

He went into the kitchen, opened the refrigerator, and his heart sank.

A little piece of caciocavallo, four passuluna olives, five sardines in oil, and a sprig of celery. Well, at least Adelina had bought some fresh bread.

He opened the oven. And howled like a wolf with joy. Eggplant parmesan, done up just right, enough for four!

He lit the oven to heat it up, went out on the veranda, and set the table, choosing a special bottle of wine. He then waited for the eggplant to get nice and hot, then brought it to the table directly in the casserole, not bothering to transfer it to a plate.

When he finished it an hour and a half later, there was no need even to wash the casserole. He'd carefully cleaned it out with the bread, and the sauce was a wonder to taste.

He got up, cleared the table, and went and got the letter and a pen, then sat back down on the bench.

Three times three
is not thirty-three

Montalbano wrote down the number 9.

and six times six
is not sixty-six.

He wrote 36.

The figure thus obtained
another number shall ordain.

9 plus 36 made 45.

Add your age to the raffle
and the riddle unravel.

He was fifty-seven, and the result was the number 9364557. A telephone number, clearly. Without an area code, which implied that it was from the province of Montelusa.

So, what now?

Should he drop the whole silly game or carry on?

Curiosity easily got the better of him. After all, these were days where he had plenty of time to waste. It had been years since he was last able to blow off whole days. He got up, went into the dining room, and dialed the number.

"Hello?" said a male voice.

"Montalbano here."

"Is that you, Inspector?"

"I'm sorry, who am I speaking to?"

"Don't you recognize me? It's Tano, the barman at the Marinella Bar."

"I'm sorry, Tano, but since I . . ."

"What are you gonna do, are you gonna drop by?"

"What for?"

"To pick up the letter somebody left for you yesterday. They didn't tell you?"

"No."

"If you like, I could bring it over to your house, but it wouldn't be before one o'clock. Closing time, you know."

"No, thanks, I'll come by in about half an hour."

Before going out, he checked to see how much whisky there was in the house. Half a bottle. While he was at it, he might as well buy another.

He'd miscalculated the distance. To get to the Marinella Bar on foot it actually took him forty minutes.

When he walked in, Tano was setting the telephone down.

"If you'd got here a minute earlier, you coulda talked to 'em."

"To whom?"

"To the person that left the letter for you."

He seriously doubted that person felt like talking to him.

"Somebody called?"

"Just now."

"What'd they want?"

"They wanted to know if you'd come by to pick up the letter, and I told 'em you'd be here any minute."

"What kind of voice did he have?"

"Why, don't you know 'im?"

"No."

"It sounded to me like a fairly old man. But he mighta been fakin' it. He didn't say hello, nothin', he just wanted to know if you'd come by. Here's the letter."

He took it out from under the bar and handed it to him.

The envelope was exactly the same as the one he'd already received, with the name written in the same way as on the other, and with the same sort of heading: *Treasure Hunt*. He put it in his jacket pocket, ordered the bottle of whisky, took it, paid, and left. It took him almost an hour to get back. He walked slowly, wanting to enjoy the outing. Back at home, he settled back on the bench and opened the envelope. Inside was half a sheet of paper with a poem.

Now that you've entered the game
you have no choice but to progress.
Following this feeble flame
of mine, try now to guess.

Tell me, my good Inspector,
where does the street become tight
and turn into a wheel, and vector
straight from the plain to the heights?

If you can guess, go without further ado,
travel the whole road and you'll see

a place quite familiar to you
and another that may be the key.

Aside from the fact that from a metrical point of view, the lines really stank, he didn't understand a thing. No, actually, there was one thing he understood. That the person writing to him was a pretentious asshole. This was clear from the phrase "my good Inspector," which seemed to come from someone who thought of himself as God in heaven at the very least.

Whatever the case, he would never manage to solve the riddle that same night. He needed a map. Therefore the best thing was to go to bed.

He didn't exactly get a good night's sleep. He had strange dreams in which inflatable dolls were telling him riddles that he was unable to solve.

Gallo came by to pick him up at eight-thirty.

"Do me a favor, Gallo. After you drop me off, go to city hall and ask them for a topographical map of Vigàta. Or better yet, a street map. If they haven't got any, ask for a copy of the latest town-planning scheme. Or whether they have one of those views of the whole town, shot from above."

"Ah, Chief, Chief!" Catarella exclaimed the moment the inspector set foot in the station. "'Ere's a jinnelman a-waitin' f'yiz an' 'e wants a talk t'yiz poissonally in poisson."

"Who is he?"

" 'E sez 'is name izzat 'e's called Girolammo Cacazzone."

"Are we sure that's his real name?"

"Who's asposta be sure, Chief? Me, youse, or Cacazzone?"

"You."

"As fer misself, I's assolutely soitin! In fact, mebbe Cacazzone hisself ain't so soitin as' I's soitin!"

"All right, show him in."

Two minutes later a man of about eighty appeared with
hair completely white, because of his age, no doubt, but
mostly because he was an albino. Medium height, shabby suit,
dusty shoes, and the look of someone who's perpetually out
of his element, even in the bathroom of his own home. For
his age he seemed pretty well preserved, except for the fact
that his hands trembled.

"I'm Girolamo Cavazzone."

How could you go wrong?

"Did you wish to speak to me?"

"Yes."

"Please sit down and tell me what you have to say."

The man looked around with the bewildered air of one
who, awakened from a leaden sleep, can't figure out where
he is.

"Well?" the inspector exhorted him.

"Ah, yes, right. Excuse me. I've taken the liberty of disturbing you to ask you for a word of advice. You may not be
the most suitable person, but since I didn't know who to—"

"I'm listening," Montalbano cut him off.

"You, I'm sure, yes, you don't know it, but I am the nephew of Gregorio and Caterina Palmisano."

"Oh, really? I wasn't aware they had any relatives."

"We haven't seen each other for some twenty years. Family matters, inheritance . . . I don't know whether . . . In short, my mother didn't inherit a thing; everything went to the other two children, Gregorio and Caterina, and so . . ."

"Listen, please try to organize your thoughts."

"Forgive me . . . I'm so mortified. . . . My maternal grandparents, Angelo and Matilde Palmisano, had a daughter, Antonia, one year after getting married. Bear in mind that when she had Antonia, Nonna Matilde wasn't yet nineteen years old. Then Antonia, when she was eighteen, married Mario Cavazzone, and I was born. But then eighteen years after she'd had Antonia, Nonna Matilde unexpectedly had a son, Gregorio. She was thirty-seven at the time. And then Caterina came along. I'm not sure I've made myself clear."

"You've made yourself perfectly clear," said Montalbano, who at some point had completely lost the thread, but he didn't feel like hearing the whole genealogy repeated.

"And so, being the closest relative, I want you to tell me whether . . . with things as they are . . . since, apparently, things . . . but, of course, all in strict accordance with the law . . ."

"I'm sorry, but what 'things' are you talking about?"

"It's just that . . . I don't want to seem like someone taking advantage of . . . misfortune is always misfortune, for

Heaven's sake, and must be respected. There. But since . . .
legally speaking, of course, the implication . . ."

He stopped, took a breath, then blurted out:

"Couldn't they perhaps be considered dead?"

"Who?"

"My aunt and uncle, Gregorio and Caterina Palmisano."

"They're crazy, they're not dead."

"But they're not in full possession of their faculties, and
therefore . . ."

"Listen, Signor Cacazzone . . ." Montalbano said in ex-
asperation, purposely getting the name wrong.

"Cavazzone."

"Can we talk straight? You've come to me to ask me if
there's any chance you could inherit the possessions of your
aunt and uncle, who, though still alive, could be declared not
in full possession of their faculties. Is that right?"

"Well, in a certain sense . . ."

"No, Signor Cavazzone, that's the only sense possible.
And so my answer is that I don't know the first thing about
such matters. You should see a lawyer. Good day."

He didn't even hold out his hand. That old octogenarian
with one foot in the grave, who wanted to scavenge the lives
of a wretched pair of crazies, had deeply disturbed him.

The man stood up, more bewildered than when he'd
come in.

"Good day," he said.

And he left.

"They haven't got any maps of Vigàta at city hall," said Gallo, coming in. "And no street guides or aerial photographs, either."

"So what have they got? Anything?"

"They have the new town planning design—six big sheets that cover the whole town—but since the plan hasn't been fully approved yet, they're not allowed to grant any public requisitioning of it."

"You mean the public can't request to see it?"

"No, Chief, they said 'public requisitioning.'"

"And what does 'public requisitioning' mean?"

"Asking for a copy."

Another word to add to his list.

"An' you have to put in an explicit request for it, in writing and on the letterhead stationery of a qualified authority."

"And what would be an example of such authority?"

"Well, you, for example."

"All right, but qualified for what?"

"Maybe for being an authority."

"All right, I'll write you the request and you can take it in to them."

"Chief, 'at'd be Signura Cirribicciò's boy onna line."

It must be Pasquale, Adelina's son, a known ne'er-do-well and thief who spent most of his time going in and out of jail.

Despite the fact that the inspector had arrested him several times, he was so fond of Montalbano that he had asked him to be his own son's godfather, which had provoked a spat with Livia, who, with her northern mind-set, couldn't grasp how a police inspector could have the son of an ex-convict as his godson.

"Okay, put him on."

"Hello, Inspector, 'iss is Pasquale Cirrinciò."

"What is it, Pasquà?"

"I wannitt a tell ya I took my mutha to the hospital."

"Oh my God! What happened?"

"She got a big scare at yer house."

"Why, what happened?"

"Well, she needed to git a broom, an' when she open the closet door, two dead ladies fell on toppa her. At lease 'at's what she tought, an' she hadda fit."

Matre santa, the dolls! He'd forgotten to leave a note to warn Adelina!

"They're not . . . They're not dead ladies, they're . . ."

"I know, Inspector. My mutha come runnin' out the house screamin' like a banshee an' then she fainted. When she woke up, she call' me onna cell phone. An' so I raced over there to git 'er, but before takin' 'er to the hospital, I went inside a have a look a' wha' was the story. Y'know what I mean? 'Cause if it was a coupla real dead bodies ya wannit a hide or sum'm, I coulda given ya a hand . . ."

"To do what?"

"What do you mean, to do what? To get the hassle offa

ya hands. Get rid o' the bodies. Iss pretty easy a do nowadays, wit' acid."

What the fuck was this kid thinking? That he was keeping two corpses at home, waiting for the right opportunity to get rid of them? Better change the subject, otherwise he would end up having to thank the guy for his generous offer of complicity in the concealment of two corpses.

"And how's Adelina now?"

"She's gotta fever of a hunnert 'n' four. An' she's worried 'bout ya. She tol' me to let ya know she coun't cook nuthin' for dinner for ya tonight."

"All right, thanks for calling. Give your mother a hug for me and my best wishes."

The youth didn't respond, but was still on the line.

"Was there anything else, Pasquà?"

"Yessir, Inspector, if I could, I'd like a say sumthin'."

"Go right ahead."

"I jess wannit a say that, a man like you, livin' all alone an' all, an' with yer girlfrien' who don't come see ya too often, well, I jess wannit a say iss logickal that . . ."

"Yes?"

"Iss logickal that every now 'n' then ya got certain needs . . ."

"But I've already got your mother to help me out."

"The kinda help I's talkin' 'bout my mama can't give ya . . ."

"So what are you talking about, then?"

"Now, don' take offince or nuthin', but if ya wanna nice-lookin' girl, alls ya gotta do is gimme a ring an' I'll fine one for ya, instead o' usin' them dolls, ya know? A nice-looking Russian or Romanian girl, or Moltavian, whatever ya like best. Blond, black, anyting ya want. Guaranteed clean and healthy. An' free o' charge, since it's you. Y'unnastan' what I'm sayin'? Ya want me to look into it?"

Dumbfounded, now that he grasped what Pasquale was offering, Montalbano was speechless. He couldn't even manage to open his mouth.

"Hello, Inspector? Can ya hear me?"

He hung up the receiver. That was all he needed! And now who was going to convince Adelina and her son that he wasn't sleeping with inflatable dolls?! He sat there for a good five minutes, unable to do anything except curse.

5

Gallo returned about half an hour later.

"All taken care of."

"So where are the papers?"

"They have to photocopy them."

"And does it take so long?"

"Chief, don't you know what people working in government offices are like? They wanted to give me them tomorrow, but I managed to persuade them to have them ready by four o'clock this afternoon. But they want ten euros. Six just for the copying, and four for the rush."

"Here you go."

Fucking treasure hunt.

And in the meantime he had to shell out ten euros. The mysterious riddler would have to be patient. He might even have to wait till tomorrow.

Montalbano dawdled about the office until lunchtime. By the time he went out he was dying of boredom.

How was it possible that there weren't any more serious robberies, shootouts, or attempted murders? Had they all become saints?

At Enzo's he stuffed his guts, partly because he had a good appetite despite the eggplant parmesan of the night before, partly because he wanted to make it up to Enzo for disappointing him the last time. A full battery of antipasti, in the sense that he had a sampling of every antipasto on the menu, *spaghetti alle vongole veraci* (and truly *veraci*), and five striped surmullet (and truly striped).

It occurred to him that Enzo, in the kitchen, had no imagination. He always made the same dishes. But the ingredients were always extremely fresh and Enzo could cook like a god. Montalbano liked a little imagination in the kitchen, but only in the hands of a culinary artist. Otherwise it was best to remain within the bounds of normality.

And this time he had to take his walk along the jetty, all the way to the lighthouse. He sat down on the flat rock and stayed about twenty minutes, relishing the smell of algae and *lippo*, that sort of aromatic green slime that covered the waterline of the rock and teemed with tiny little sea animals. Then he went back to the office.

Shortly after four o'clock, Gallo brought him the photocopies of the town planning scheme. Six enormous sheets, rolled up and numbered.

No, he couldn't bring them home to Marinella. He already had the two dolls there. All that paper would only add to the confusion.

Taking a quick look around his office he calculated that if he moved the two armchairs and small sofa out of the way, he could create enough space to lay the six sheets out on the floor, lining them up in sequence, according to their numbering.

He pushed the furniture to the walls, unrolled the first sheet, and spread it out on the floor.

And immediately the problems started, because the goddamn sheet of paper didn't want to stay in place and simply rolled itself back up. And so he grabbed the magnifying glass that was on the desk, three different instruction manuals, the penal code, two boxes of paper clips, a box of pens—in short, everything that might serve as a paperweight but didn't take up too much space—and after some fifteen minutes of cursing the saints, he had managed to spread the sheets out in the proper order, holding them down with a variety of strategically placed objects.

But the whole turned out to be too big for him to look at while standing over it. So he grabbed a chair and climbed up on it.

Then he took the poem out of his pocket.

But how was it that Mimì Augello always happened to come in at moments like this?

"What movie is playing tonight? *Superman*? *Spider-Man*? *007: From Vigàta with Love*? Or is this going to be a speech to the nation?" he asked.

Montalbano didn't answer, and Mimì left, shaking his head.

Surely, thought the inspector, *he's convinced I'm getting more senile with each day that goes by. Why doesn't he just worry about himself? He's the one who's forced to wear glasses, even though he's a lot younger . . .*

The first quatrain of the poem served no purpose. The directions didn't start until the second stanza, with the words: *where does the street become tight.*

He got down from the chair, grabbed a pen and a sheet of paper, then climbed back up.

But he couldn't see much. The sun had shifted and there wasn't much light coming in through the window anymore.

He got down again, turned on the overhead light as well as the desk lamp, which he shone on the papers. Then he climbed back up on the chair. The desk lamp wasn't aimed properly.

He got down, positioned it better, then climbed back up. The telephone rang.

He got down, cursing and laughing, feeling as if he were in a Beckett play.

"Ahh Chief, Chief! Ahh Chief!"

Usually Catarella reserved this Greek-choral exordium for telephone calls from the commissioner, the supreme deity, when Zeus manifested himself from Olympus.

"What is it?"

And indeed.

" 'At'd be the C'mishner 'izzoner 'oo wants a talk t'yiz immidiotly!"

"Put him on."

"Montalbano? What is this business?"

"What business, Mr. Commissioner?"

"Dr. Arquà has sent me a detailed report."

He said he'd do it, and he did it, the motherfucking bastard. Let's pretend to know nothing about it.

"A report on what, sir?"

"On your request for the Forensic Department's intervention."

"Ah, yes."

"According to Dr. Arquà, you either wanted to play a silly joke on him, his team, Dr. Tommaseo, and Dr. Pasquano . . ."

Jesus, so many doctors! More than in a hospital!

". . . or you are no longer able to tell the difference between a dead body and an inflatable doll."

Montalbano decided he needed to summon legalese-bureaucratese to the rescue again *immidiotly*, as Catarella would say.

"Whereas, concerning the second part of the report drafted and just now submitted to you by Dr. Arquà, wherein I am apprised of being the object, not of any circumstantiated impugnment, but of a base and gratuitous insinuation that nevertheless proves prejudicial in my regard, I intend to avail myself of the right to a defense accorded me by august institutional authority in the face of the abovementioned—"

"Listen, it's just a matter of—"

"Please let me finish."

Dry and brusque, like someone who has suffered an offense to his dignity and honor.

"As concerns instead the first part, wherein the aforementioned doctor ascribes the occurrence in question to some carnivalesque impulse on my part, I find myself in the position, my better sense notwithstanding, of being forced to inform the cognizant jurisdictional authority of its easily demonstrated personal, incontrovertible accountability in the matter."

"*Its* meaning whose, excuse me?"

"*Its* meaning yours, Mr. Commissioner."

"Mine?!"

"Yessir, yours. With all due and unmitigated respect, sir, I would call to your attention that in accepting the Arquà report for perscrutation and then demanding an explanation of me, you effectively impugn me for what is a prejudicially foregone conclusion on your part, and in so doing endorse the hypothesis that I am a person capable of such silly jokes, thereby junking, in a single stroke, a distinguished, exemplary career spanning more than two decades and achieved through sacrifice and absolute devotion to work—"

"Good God, Montalbano!"

"—through hardship and honesty, with never a scam, never a kickback, irrespective of the contingency, notwithstanding the failure to securitize the—"

"Montalbano, stop it! I didn't mean in any way to offend you!"

Now it was time to pull out the cracking voice, on the verge of tears.

"And yet you did! Perhaps without meaning to, but you did! And I am so pained, so aggrieved that—"

"Listen, Montalbano, hear me out. I really had no idea it would upset you so. Let's drop the whole thing for now. Next time we have a chance, we can talk about it again, okay? But calmly, without getting excited, all right?"

"Thank you, Mr. Commissioner."

He congratulated himself. He'd put on a good performance, extricating himself without wasting too much time. He called Catarella.

"I'm not here for anyone," he told him.

And he climbed back up on the chair and started to study the sheets, sector by sector, taking notes.

After half an hour or so, it turned out that sixty percent of the streets in Vigàta narrowed at some point of their course. But there were only three that did so in an especially emphatic way. He wrote down their names and then proceeded to the second clue, the one that said that the street turned *into a wheel*.

How the hell could a street turn into a wheel?

Unless it meant that at that point there was a bus terminus that he was supposed to take. He reexamined the three streets.

Then he suddenly noticed that one of them, Via Garibaldi, to be precise, after narrowing towards the end like the trousers men used to wear, merged into a roundabout.

That must be the wheel the poem was talking about!

Then, after circling the roundabout, there was a street, Via dei Mille, which climbed up the hill where there was a cemetery halfway up the slope, and then continued through the newly built districts north of the town. He was sure he'd found it.

He looked at his watch: five-thirty. Therefore he had all the time in the world. Then he cursed the saints, remembering that he wouldn't be getting his car back from the mechanic's until the following morning. But there was no harm in trying.

"Montalbano here. I was wondering whether my car—"

"In about half an hour you can come an' pick 'er up, Inspector."

Who was the patron saint of auto mechanics? He didn't know. So, just to be sure, he thanked them all.

He went out and told Catarella he was leaving and wouldn't be back that evening.

"But tomorrow inna mornin' you'll be back, Chief?"

"Not to worry, Cat. See you tomorrow."

Christ, if he were ever to die, Catarella was liable to die, too, of sadness, as sometimes happened with certain dogs. And would Livia die of sadness if he were gone?

"*Shall we turn the question around? If Livia passed away, would you die of sadness?*" Montalbano Two asked obnoxiously.

He preferred not to answer.

Forty-five minutes later, he was taking the roundabout and coming out onto Via dei Mille.

Passing the cemetery, he continued driving uphill between two unending walls of concrete, gray tenement houses rather like a cross between a Mexican high-security prison and a bunker-style loony bin for stark raving mad murderers conceived in some stark raving mad murderer's nightmare. For some reason it was called low-income housing.

According to those architectural geniuses, working-class people were supposed live in homes where the moment you stuck the key in the door and went inside for the first time, the walls began to crumble before your eyes like underground frescoes when the air and light come in.

Small rooms so dark you had to keep the lights turned on at all times and it felt like northern Sweden in winter. The architects' single great achievement was that they had actually managed to cancel out the Sicilian sun.

When the inspector was a little boy his uncle used to take him sometimes to the house of a friend who had some land in that area, and he remembered that on the right-hand side of that street, at the time a dirt road, it was all a dense grove of majestic Saracen olive trees, and on the left, an expanse of vineyards as far as the eye could see.

And now only cement. He started insulting them all in his mind, architects, engineers, surveyors, contractors, and masons, with a rage so irrational that he could feel the blood thumping in his temples.

"But why do I let it get to me so much?" he asked himself.

True, the destruction of nature, the death of good taste, the prevalence of ugliness were not only harmful, they were offensive, too. But it was clear that a good part of his rage was simply due to the fact that at a certain age you become intolerant and don't let a single thing slide. Further proof that he was getting old.

The road continued up the hill, but now on either side of the road there were small homes without pretension, luckily, with little gardens in back where chickens and dogs circulated freely. Then, all at once, the little houses disappeared and the road continued between two dry-walls and then, about a hundred yards ahead, suddenly ended.

Montalbano stopped and got out.

It wasn't true, actually, that the road ended; it was only the asphalt that did, because from that point forward the road turned into the dirt track of old, all the way down into the valley. He'd reached the very top of the hill and stood there a few moments, enjoying the panorama.

Behind him the sea, before him the distant town of Gallotta, perched atop a hill, to the right the ridge of Monserrato, which divided the territory of Vigàta from that of Montelusa. Not many patches of green. Nowadays hardly anyone worked the land anymore, a waste of effort and money.

And what now? Where was he supposed to go? In the spot where he found himself, at the top of the hill, not only were there no houses, but there wasn't a living soul about.

travel the whole road and you'll see
a place quite familiar to you

So said the poem, whose directions he had followed. He'd traveled the whole road, but there wasn't anything familiar to him. Was this some kind of joke?

About ten yards from the road stood a wooden shack, about ten feet by ten, in bad shape, and it certainly wasn't familiar to him. At any rate it was the only place where he might ask for information.

It wasn't really a proper lane that led to the shed, but rather a dirt path barely showing any sign of the passage of man. To see it you had to study the ground very carefully, indicating that it wasn't trod on very often.

Montalbano took the path to the closed front door. He knocked, but no one answered. Pressing his ear to the wood, between planks, he heard nothing at all. By this point it was clear the shack was uninhabited.

So what to do now? Should he force open the door or turn back and admit defeat?

"Let's go for broke," he said.

He went back to the car, took out a monkey wrench, and returned to the hut. Since the door wasn't flush with the jamb, he stuck the wrench in the gap and used it as a lever. The wood was very damp and broke on the third try. Two kicks were enough, and the lock fell to the floor on the inside. Montalbano opened the door and went in.

There was no furniture, not even a chair or stool. Nothing.

But the inspector remained paralyzed, mouth open, throat suddenly dry, and broke into a cold sweat.

Because there wasn't an inch of wall space that wasn't covered with photographs of him. So that was why the poem said the place would be familiar to him.

Finally managing to move, he went up to the wall in front of him to have a better look at them. They weren't exactly photographs, but computer printouts of the images that TeleVigàta had broadcast.

Him talking to Fazio, him starting his climb up the firemen's ladder, him coming down after Gregorio Palmisano had shot his gun, him climbing back up, stopping halfway, resuming his climb, and leaping over the balustrade . . . On every wall in the hut the same images were repeated. But a white envelope stood out in the middle of the central wall, attached with a piece of adhesive tape. He tore it off angrily, so that five or six of the photographs fell to the floor. He grabbed one at random, stuck it in his jacket pocket together with the envelope, and left.

"Wha'ssa story, Chief? You back? You tol' me y'wasn't comin' back," said Catarella, half surprised, half pleased.

"Are you sorry I am?"

Montalbano had changed his mind in the car. Catarella nearly had a heart attack.

"Whatcha sayin', Chief? If y'ask me, whinniver y'appear 'ere poissonally in poisson, I almos' feel like gittin' down on my knees!"

For a split second Montalbano had a horrendous vision of himself clad in a light-blue cloak like Our Lady of Fatima.

"I need you to explain something for me."

Catarella staggered for a second, as if he'd just been clubbed in the head. Too many emotions in too few seconds.

"Me . . . asplain t'yiz? Asplain? You kiddin' me?"

The inspector pulled out of his pocket the photograph from the hut and shoved it under Catarella's nose. It showed him putting his foot down on the firemen's ladder with what wasn't exactly an air of nonchalance.

"What is this?" he asked.

Catarella gave him a confused look.

"'Ass you, Chief! Dontcha rec'nize yisself?"

"I didn't ask you *who* that is, but *what*!" said Montalbano, pinching the sheet of paper between his thumb and index finger.

"Iss paper," Catarella replied.

Montalbano cursed, but only in his mind. He didn't want to make Catarella upset, but just get him to explain a few things about "pewters."

"Is that a photograph or not?"

Catarella took it out of his hands.

"If I mays," he said.

He studied it for a few moments, then gave his sentence.

"'Iss is a photaraff 'ass not rilly a photaraff."

"Good, good! Go on."

"'Iss pitcher wadn't took wit' a camera, but transferrated from a VHS to a pewter ann' 'enn prinnit."

"Splendid! And how did it get onto the VHS?"

"'Ey musta riccorded the pogram on TeleVigàta."

"And how did they make the photographs?"

"By 'ookin' up a viddeo riccorder to a priph'ral of a pewter, a priph'ral 'ass called a viddeo 'quisition."

The inspector didn't understand a goddamn thing about the last part, but he'd found out what he'd wanted to know.

"Cat, you're a god!"

Catarella suddenly turned bright red, opened his arms, spreading his fingers, and did a half-pirouette. Whenever Montalbano praised him, he got so puffed up he became like a peacock spreading its tail.

As soon as he got back home, he remembered that there was nothing to eat, and he felt a little hungry. It would have been a mistake to skip supper because, later in the night, that little bit of hunger would turn into out-and-out ravenousness. He pulled the letter out of his pocket, still unopened, along with the photograph, set them both down on the table, went to splash a little water on his face, and then remained undecided about what to do about dinner, since he didn't feel like going back to Enzo's after having been there for lunch.

The telephone rang.

"Hello?"

"How long has it been since we last saw each other?" said a beautiful female voice that he recognized immediately.

"Since the days of Rachele," he replied. "Have any news of her?"

"Yes, she's doing well. I was just admiring your brave deeds on TV the other day and I felt like seeing you again."

"That can be arranged."

"Are you free this evening?"

"Yes."

"All right, then, I'll come by in half an hour. In the meantime try to think of a nice place to take me out to dinner."

He was pleased to hear from Ingrid, his Swedish friend, confidante, and sometimes accomplice.

To make that half hour go by, he thought he would read the new instructions for the treasure hunt. He picked up the envelope but then put it back down almost immediately. There might be something in it that would upset him. Reading it before going out to eat was therefore out of the question, since there was the risk it might make him lose his appetite.

All at once he remembered what had happened with Adelina, and he went and opened the closet to check on the dolls. They were gone.

Apparently Pasquale had put them somewhere else. But where? They weren't in the kitchen. He opened the armoire, but they weren't there either. Want to bet he took them home with him? Perhaps the best thing was to give him a ring, so he could also get an update on Adelina.

6

Pasquale's wife answered the phone and told him her husband had gone out and would be back in about an hour.

"Should I have him call you?"

"No, thank you. I'm going out now and won't be back till late."

"Should I tell him anything?"

"Well, yes."

He had to say it in a roundabout way so that she wouldn't understand what he was talking about . . .

"Tell him I urgently need those things we were talking about, and to call me tomorrow morning."

Then he went and sat on the veranda to smoke a cigarette.

When he saw Ingrid in the doorway, he did a double take.

How was it that the years didn't pass for that woman? The gears of time had jammed for her. In fact, she looked even younger to him than the last time he'd seen her, and more than a year had gone by. She was dressed the same way as usual, jeans, blouse, and sandals. And she was as elegant as if she were wearing a designer dress.

They hugged warmly. Ingrid didn't use perfume, she didn't need to, because her skin smelled like just-picked apricots.

"Want to come in?"

"Not now, maybe later. Have you decided where to go?"

"Yes, there's a restaurant on the shore, at Montereale, where—"

"The one with the antipasti? I know it. Let's take my car."

He couldn't figure out what make Ingrid's car was, but it was the sort of model she really liked. A two-seater, and flat as a filet of sole.

Four-wheeled, very fast sole. With another woman at the wheel, he might not have been so ready to climb aboard that sort of missile, but he trusted her driving. In fact, when she still lived in Sweden, Ingrid had been a race-car mechanic.

It took her twenty minutes to get to the restaurant, a distance that would have taken Montalbano a good forty-five. When she drove, Ingrid preferred not to talk. But every so often she turned to look at Montalbano, smiling and lightly stroking his leg.

They sat down at the table closest to the sea, about twenty yards from the beach. The restaurant was famous for the quantity and quality of its antipasti, to the point that almost all its customers skipped the first course. Which was what they decided to do, too. They also ordered a bottle of chilled white wine.

As they were waiting for the first antipasti, they used the time to chat a little. Ingrid knew that once he had a plate in front of him, Montalbano only liked to open his mouth to eat.

"How's your husband doing?"

"I never see the guy! Ever since he got elected, he barely comes to Montelusa once every couple of months."

"Don't you ever go to Rome to see him?"

"Whatever for?"

"Well, you *are* still husband and wife. . . ."

"Come on, Salvo, you know very well that it's only a formality. And, anyway, I like things this way."

"Any new loves?"

"Is this an official interrogation?"

"Of course not, it's just to make conversation."

"All right, just to make conversation, the answer is no."

"So, no men for the past year?"

"Are you kidding? I guess that, like a good Catholic, you think a woman should only sleep with a man she's in love with?"

"If I was so Catholic as you say, I would reply that a woman should only sleep with the man she's married to."

"Good God, how boring!"

The waiter arrived carrying the first six dishes delicately balanced in his arms.

After twelve different copious appetizers and two bottles of wine, while waiting for the main course, a mixed grill of fish, they resumed their conversation.

"And what about you?" Ingrid asked.

"Me what?"

"Still faithful to Livia, with an occasional exception?"

"Yes."

"You mean yes to fidelity or yes to the exceptions?"

"Fidelity."

"You mean that after Rachele—"

"Nothing."

"Not even a little temptation?"

"As for temptations, I have those all the time."

"Really? So how do you resist? Do you just say a little prayer and the devil runs away?"

"Come on, don't mock me."

"I'm not mocking you. On the contrary. I admire you. Sincerely."

"You used to ask fewer questions."

"I guess I'm just becoming more and more Italian and nosey about others. Tell me, does it take a lot out of you?"

"Does what take a lot out of me?"

"Resisting temptation."

"Sometimes, yes. But lately less and less. It must be my age."

Ingrid looked at him and then started laughing with gusto.

"What's so funny?"

"This business about age. You're totally wrong, you know. Age has very little to do with these things. I can tell you from personal experience. There are thirty-year-olds who seem like they're seventy, in this respect, and vice versa."

The grilled fish arrived, along with another bottle. When they were done, Montalbano asked her if she wanted a whisky.

"Yes, I do. But at your place."

As soon as Ingrid turned up the driveway to his house, she asked:

"Were you expecting someone?"

"No."

He too had noticed the strange car parked outside the front door.

When they pulled up beside it, out of the other car emerged a girl of about twenty, nearly six feet tall and gorgeous, blond, wearing a miniskirt up to her pubis and a little too much makeup. They got out of their car too.

"Montalbano?"

"Yes?"

"I ring doorbell but nobody answer. So I think you out but come back later."

Montalbano was flummoxed. Who was this? What did she want?

"Listen . . ."

"Nobody tell me you want with three people. I can do, but only with you. I don't like with other woman. But she can watch."

"Well, if that's the problem . . ." said Ingrid, rather angrily, "I'll leave right now. Bye, Salvo, have fun."

She made as if to get back into her car, but didn't, because Montalbano grabbed her arm as he turned towards the girl.

"Listen, signorina, this must be some kind of mistake, I never—"

"I understand. You pick her up and like her. No problem. I go."

Montalbano let go of Ingrid's arm, went up to the girl and said in a low voice:

"I'll pay you anyway. How much do I owe?"

"All paid. Ciao."

She got in the car and left, driving back up the driveway in reverse.

Montalbano, still half confused, opened the front door, and Ingrid followed him inside, not saying a word. When he opened the French door to the veranda, she went outside and sat down, still silent. He got a bottle of whisky and two glasses and then sat down beside her on the bench.

Ingrid grabbed the brand-new bottle and poured herself half a glass without offering any to Montalbano.

"I don't understand why you're so upset," the inspector began, pouring himself some whisky. "After all, between us, there's—"

"Between us, my ass!"

Montalbano decided it was perhaps better to drink in silence. After a brief spell, she was the first to speak.

"Don't think I'm jealous or anything. I don't give a fuck about your women."

"So then why are you making that face?"

"Because I'm profoundly disappointed."

"About what?"

"Disappointed in you. I had no idea you could be such a hypocrite."

"What are you talking about?"

"What is this? At the restaurant you tell me there'd been no exceptions since Rachele and when we come back here there's a whore waiting for you. So I guess, for you, going with a whore doesn't constitute an exception, because you don't even consider a prostitute to be a real woman."

"Ingrid, you are totally on the wrong track! There was a misunderstanding. I can explain everything."

"You don't have to explain anything to me, and at any rate, I don't want to hear it. I'm going to the bathroom."

Man, what a mess that fucking idiot Pasquale had created! In his rage Montalbano downed a whole glass of whisky. He heard Ingrid come out of the bathroom and then, moments later, he heard her cry out.

"What's going on?"

"Nothing, nothing."

She didn't come back right away. Then she returned barefoot, holding her sandals in her hand. But she was different. Her eyes were now sparkling and she was wearing a mischievous, mocking smile.

"Way to go, Salvo!" she said, sitting back down beside him.

"Listen, I'd like to explain . . ."

"I repeat, I don't care what your explanation is. I've known many men, but never one as hypocritical as you!"

Enough about hypocrisy! But this time, when she spoke, it was clear she was about to start laughing. What was going through her head?

"At the restaurant," she resumed, "you told me it was your age that allowed you to resist temptation. But now I see you've found another way. You're such a liar, Salvo!"

She refilled her glass.

"Of course, we women have vibrators. But it's not the same thing."

What on earth was she talking about?

"But why two?" she continued. "And on top of that, they're both blond. Wouldn't it have made more sense to get one blonde and one brunette?"

At last there was light.

"Where did you find them?"

"Under your bed. I bent down to untie my sandals and . . ."

But he was no longer listening. He stood up, climbed over her, and ran to the bedroom. The two inflatable dolls were right under the bed. That asshole Pasquale had had the bright idea to hide them there. Montalbano returned to the veranda.

"All right, now you can keep guzzling that bottle while I tell you the whole story. But I want you to listen."

He told her everything, and at certain moments Ingrid was literally doubled over, her stomach hurting from laughing so hard.

When it was time to go at three in the morning, after all the whisky in the house had been drunk, Ingrid slapped herself on the forehead.

"I was about to forget! There's a friend of mine who'd like to meet you."

"An ex?"

"No, come on. He's a twenty-year-old kid, very bright. He's madly in love with me, but he admires you even more. It would make me very happy if you talked to him. His name is Arturo Pennisi."

"Tell him to give me a ring tomorrow, around noon, at the office. And to mention your name. Think you can manage to drive?"

"I hope so. I won't ask you to put me up because I've got workmen coming to the house tomorrow morning at eight. Ciao. Luv ya."

She kissed him lightly on the lips, went out, got in her car, and drove off.

Whereas around two o'clock Montalbano had started to feel sleepy, he now felt completely awake. He went and washed his face, then grabbed the envelope from before and sat back down on the veranda. This time his name wasn't on it, but only the words: *Treasure Hunt*.

Before opening it, however, he tried to imagine what kind of man might organize this sort of game, and why. He knew from experience that if somebody asks you two questions in a row, it's always best to answer the second one first, because the answer you give to the second question will help you in some way to answer the first.

Thus: Why this so-called treasure hunt? What interest did the guy have in organizing it? Any practical or economic interest was out of the question. Normally a treasure hunt involved the participation of a number of people, either as individuals or in groups, whereas here it seemed that there was one and only one contestant: him. And, in fact, the envelope containing the first note had borne his name. On top of that, the first line of the second stanza had called him out directly:

Tell me, my good Inspector . . .

And on top of this, hadn't the walls of the hut been papered with photographs of him?

There could be no doubt, therefore, that this was more than a game: it was a personal challenge. Addressed not to Montalbano the man, but to Montalbano the cop.

Now who would challenge a cop? Either another cop, as in, say, a competition of skills to see who could solve a case first, or a person with a certain kind of mentality. Not necessarily a criminal mentality, to be sure, but certainly someone with his head not screwed on entirely straight, who wanted to show that he was better and smarter than the cop.

And who wanted to let the inspector know indirectly that, if he felt like it, he was capable of anything, because at any rate Montalbano would never be able to track him down because he wasn't up to the task, was not on the same level of intelligence.

So one had to wonder whether such a man would continue to keep within the parameters of a game created just to pass the time, or, at a certain point, take it up a dangerous notch or two. Test the limits of the law, or even go beyond them.

QED: by answering the second question he had answered, in part, the first: who was this man?

The question, of course, did not presume it would receive a full answer, with first and last names.

It had to be put more precisely: What kind of man was this? In short, he had to create a profile of him.

And here he felt like laughing. He'd seen so many American movies where there was a psychologist working with the police who would draw up profiles of unknown murderers. And these movie psychologists were always brilliant. With a serial killer they'd never seen before they could manage to tell you how tall he was, his age, whether he was married or single, what bad things had happened to him when he was five, and whether he drank beer or Coca-Cola. And they were always right on target.

But it was best not to stray too far afield. It couldn't be an old man he was dealing with, because an old man would not have known how to use the high-tech tools needed to make those photographs. It had to be someone between twenty and sixty years of age. In other words, half the country. Intelligent, proud, given to considering himself so much sharper and shrewder than others that he felt in some way able to win whatever sort of game he might wish to play. In other words, a dangerous man.

Wouldn't it therefore be better to cut short the treasure hunt, instead of continuing the challenge? No, it would be a mistake. He would surely take the inspector's withdrawal as an insult and probably avenge himself somehow. How? By doing something outrageous, something that would force Montalbano to keep playing. No, it was better not to take that chance.

He grabbed the envelope, opened it, and took out the note.

The usual little poem that made you want to throw up, which even an illiterate street minstrel would have felt too embarrassed to write.

I can see at this stuff you're an ace!
You quickly found the right place!

11-6-7 / B-6-1-4-18 / 3-4 / 1-4-7-6-16-16-1-18-6-4-7 /
5-2-8-M-9-2-15
D-12-6-5-4-7 / 3-16-W-3-11-5 / B-13-1-4-18 / 18-12-
12-D / 16-9-2-15!

1-2-3 / 6-3-X-1 / 16-6-3 / 14-16-12 / 8-16-6-1 /
2-5-V-3 / 1-16 / 10-16-16-K / F-16-7,
9-1-6-6 / B-3 / 19-3-6-9-V-3-7-3-19 / 7-9-18-2-1 /
1-16 / 14-16-12-7 / 19-16-16-7.

The manner will surely surprise you,
but that's our game, and it will continue.

Man, what a pain in the ass! What was this, the *Settimana Enigmistica* or something? A message in code? Reserved for the privileged few who could decipher it? And those first two lines of verse—if you could really call them that—displayed about the same level of poetic craft as that old television commercial where the robot says to the housewife:

Now that I know all your wishes,
do you mind if I do the dishes?

Montalbano still didn't feel sleepy, despite all the wine and whisky he'd guzzled, and so he went into the bathroom, got undressed, washed himself, put his shirt back on and, still in his underpants, grabbed a pen and a sheet of paper, returned to the veranda, and sat back down.

If the author of the poem, for lack of a better term, kept to the general rules of puzzles, then each number repeated in the lines should correspond to one same letter, also repeated.

It was clear that all the vowels and consonants written in

code should be contained in the two couplets not in code, that is, the first and the last.

He got down to work on the start of the poem. He wrote down the first line and underneath it, as a test, he wrote numbers in sequence, starting at 1, corresponding to the appearance of each new letter.

I   can   see   at   this   stuff
y o u're   an   ace
1 / 2 3 4 / 5 6 6 / 3 7 / 7 8 1 5 / 5 7 9 10 10 /
11 12 9 13 6 / 3 4 / 3 2 6

Since the first line of the second couplet contained four groups of numbers separated by slashes, this must mean that the line was made up of four words. He then copied out the second line of the first couplet and assigned the proper numbers.

Then he copied the first four groups of numbers in the first line of the second couplet, and under them wrote out the corresponding vowels or consonants, based on the numeration he had just established.

11 6 7 / B 6 1 4 18 / 3 4 / 1 4 7 6 16 16 1 18 6 4 7
Yet / Being / an / intelligent

He'd hit the nail on the head on the first try! Decoded, the two lines read as follows:

Yet being an intelligent schmuck
doesn't always bring good luck!

Now he took the first two groups of numbers of the third couplet and copied them down.

1-2-3 / 6-3-X-1

Under them he wrote the corresponding vowels and consonants, which yielded:

I c a   e a x i

Which didn't mean a goddamn thing, not even in Chinese or Greenlandian. But then he suddenly thought:

"Wanna bet the code of the third couplet can be found in the last two lines in clear, and I have to renumber every vowel and consonant starting with 1?"

He gave it a try. And it proved to be the right approach.

The next . . .

This time, too, he'd guessed right. He continued:

The next one you won't have to look for,
It'll be delivered right to your door.

Having deciphered the message in full, he felt a little disappointed.

He'd wasted a lot of time trying to come up with a profile of the man who wanted to take him on this treasure hunt, and the portrait that had emerged gave reason for concern. But the riddles, cryptograms, and puzzles the person had come up with were totally pedestrian, real beginners' stuff. Did he make them that way on purpose, because he considered the inspector incapable of solving more complex problems? Or was it because that was the level of their creator himself?

Whatever the case, since he had no choice but to wait for the guy to get back in touch, Montalbano got up, closed the French door, and went to bed.

7

He was awakened by the telephone. It was nine A.M.

"Hello, Inspector? Pasquale here. Wha'ss wrong, din'tcha like the girl I sent ya? Tell me azackly whatcha din't like about 'er, an' I'll sendja 'nother t'night."

Montalbano immediately remembered his embarrassment with Ingrid and felt like chewing the kid out, but he controlled himself. After all, in his own way, the guy was trying to do him a favor.

"But Pasquà, what the hell were you thinking?"

"Din't you want a girl?"

"Whatever gave you that idea?"

"Ya said it y'self, Inspector!"

"I did?! I didn't say anything over the phone! I just hung up!"

Pasquale paused for a moment, and then exclaimed:

"That's when the mistake was made!"

"What mistake?"

"My mistake, Inspector. I thought that, since you din't say nothin', you was okay wit' it. An' then you confirmed it when you called my house."

"I confirmed it?"

"Yessir, you did. My wife tol' me you said you urgently needed those things we was talkin' 'bout. So I thought you meant the girls."

Want to bet this would end up with Montalbano apologizing? Perhaps it was best to change the subject.

"How's your mother doing?"

"The fever's gone down. But then she got all these little red spots. The doctor said iss from gettin' so scared, but then they'll go away."

"All right, then, I'll be going now."

"So what am I s'posta do 'bout this?"

"About what?"

"About this stuff with the girls. Do you still need one or are you all set with the dolls?"

Montalbano saw red.

"Listen, Pasquà, I'm going to tell you once and for all. Mind your own fucking business! Got that?"

"Whatever you say, sir," said the youth, slightly offended.

The inspector couldn't very well go on keeping those goddamned dolls in his house. They were liable to create more trouble yet.

But where to put them? He thought about this for a moment and at a certain point became convinced he'd found the solution. It was so perfect, he was amazed he hadn't thought of it earlier.

He would bury them in the sand, digging a grave for them beside the veranda.

He opened the closet, grabbed a shovel, went out on the

beach, chose the spot, looked around to see if anyone was walking by, and then started digging.

It wasn't easy, because the sand, being dry and very fine, kept sliding back down and refilling the hole. After fifteen minutes of this, Montalbano took off his shirt.

It took him an hour of hard labor, but in the end he'd managed to dig a hole the right size. But he was dead tired. He must have drunk more than half a gallon of water.

He went and pulled the first doll out from under the bed, but when he was about to go through the French door, he froze and cursed the saints. A mere ten or so yards away, just opposite the veranda, there was now a family, father, mother, and two small children, who'd just got out of their car. They were setting up a large umbrella.

There was nothing to be done. They looked like they intended to stay for a while.

He carried the doll into the entrance hall, went and got the other one and put it beside her, gave himself a thorough washing, got dressed, went outside, got in the car, and backed it up as close as he could to the front door, so that he could load the dolls into it without anyone noticing. If anyone spotted him from afar, they might start yelling that he was trying to hide dead bodies in his trunk.

He realized too late, halfway to his destination, that the car in front of him was braking for a roadblock of the carabinieri up ahead. And so he was forced to stop suddenly. As a result, the car behind him slammed hard into his, and the trunk popped open. The woman driving got out in a huff, infuriated, caught a glimpse of what was in it, let out a long howl that sounded exactly like a ferryboat siren, and then fell lengthwise to the ground, unconscious.

Upon seeing the woman collapse like an empty sack, the carabinieri, having no idea what this was about, started running to the two cars with their weapons drawn and shouting to everyone not to move.

In the twinkling of an eye Montalbano, who had sprained his neck in the whiplash, as they call it, was forced to get out of the car with his hands raised.

"The woman didn't—" he began.

"Silence!"

A carabinieri corporal, who'd bent down to have a look inside the trunk, came towards the inspector, giving him dirty looks.

Meanwhile two motorists had succeeded in rousing the unconscious woman. Who, the moment she came to, leapt to her feet, pointed a finger at Montalbano, and started wailing hysterically:

"Murderer! Murderer!"

The inspector didn't know whether to laugh or cry, but he was certainly sweating bullets. Meanwhile an endless line of cars had formed behind them, and the number of onlookers getting out of their cars and running up to see what was happening was growing at the rate of five or six per second, at a rough guess.

"Listen, I can explain . . ." he said, turning towards the corporal.

The young officer raised a hand, enjoining him to remain silent.

"You're coming with us," he said.

"What for?"

"Trafficking pornographic materials."

"I'd like to explain. . . ."

"You can explain at the station!"

That was all he needed.

To be hauled into carabinieri headquarters and there, once they discovered who he was, to become the miserable butt of their jokes, to the great delight of them all . . . No, this had to be avoided at all costs. It was better to try to resolve the matter at once, even if it meant lowering himself to the now ridiculous statement, "You don't know who I am."

"Listen, I'm a chief inspector of police."

"And I'm the pope!"

"Can I get my papers?"

"Yes, but move very slowly."

By the time he got to the office his hair was standing on end from rage and a sprained neck, and his hands were trembling.

"Jeezis, Chief! Wha' happened?" Catarella asked in alarm.

"Nothing, I had a little accident. Get Fazio for me."

"Chief, what happened?" Fazio repeated upon seeing him.

"Nothing, some stupid woman bumped me from behind and the carabinieri nearly arrested me."

And he told him the whole story.

"Why don't you go have your neck looked at?"

"Later, later. This bullshit was all I needed! Listen, the two inflatable dolls are in my trunk. Have Palmisano's doll taken back to their house using the same chest as before. Then put the other one back in that chest and leave it in the garage for me."

"Okay, I'll get on that right away."

At last he was rid of those two big pains in the ass.

But he was mistaken.

Those two big pains in the ass would continue to plague him from afar. Not even King Tut's mummy was so jinxed! Half an hour or so later, in fact, he could no longer stand the pain in his neck, but among other things was in no condition to get behind the wheel of his car. And so he had Mimì Augello take him to the emergency room at Montelusa Hospital.

As a result, about an hour later he came out with a big white collar around his neck, the kind that completely immobilize it and make you look exactly like Frankenstein when you walk.

He returned to headquarters and spent a good fifteen minutes holed up in his office with the door closed, cursing the saints.

He didn't feel like going to Enzo's for lunch with that contraption around his neck. And anyway, would he even be able to eat and drink normally without dirtying his shirt and the tablecloth like a three-month-old baby or a drooling, senile geezer? He had better do a solo test at home first.

At that moment Catarella called him.

"'At'd be summon onna phone wannin' a talk t'yiz poissonally in poisson."

"Someone on behalf of another?"

Catarella didn't get the joke.

"No, iss not a half a poisson but a whole one, summon callin' for yer frenn the Sweetish lady, Signura Scioscio-strommi."

It must be the young guy Ingrid had mentioned to him.

"Put him on."

"Inspector Montalbano."

"Yes?"

"My name is Arturo Pennisi, I hope I'm not disturbing you. Ingrid said to call around this time."

"Would you like to meet me?"

"Yes."

"Have you got a car?"

"Yes."

"Would you prefer my house or my office?"

"Whatever's most convenient for you."

"Then come to the station this evening around seven. All right?"

"Excellent. Thank you so much, you're very kind."

He sounded like a nice, polite kid, this Arturo.

Since he knew what there was in the fridge from his last check—that is, next to nothing—before leaving town he stopped at a grocer's that was closing and bought fresh bread, black olives, tuna, salami, and prosciutto. When he got home, he set the table on the veranda and then sat down to eat.

The collar kept his head raised and didn't allow him to look down, which meant that he couldn't see the plate in front of him. He had to push it about a foot forward, and the problem was solved. The same went for his glass. If he wanted to fill it, he had to do so with arms extended. The third thing he realized was that he couldn't open his mouth very wide.

But these obstacles were not so great that they would prevent him from eating in public. After clearing the table, he went and lay down to catch up on the sleep he'd lost the previous night. But he had trouble finding the right position for his head. When he woke up at four o'clock, he phoned the office. There was no news, and so he took it easy.

When Catarella informed him that the kid was waiting for him, he'd already been bored stiff for a good two hours. But the dead calm had created a miracle: on his desk there were no longer several tons of papers to be signed, but barely a kilo. And he'd left that kilo there on purpose; the idea of sitting in his office with absolutely nothing to do terrified him.

Arturo Pennisi looked exactly like a twenty-year-old Harry Potter.

He even wore the same kind of glasses. He didn't seem the least bit awkward. In fact it was he who spoke first, and he got straight to the point.

"I asked Ingrid to introduce us because I'm very interested in your methods of investigation."

"Do you want to become a policeman?"

"No."

"Are you studying criminology?"

"No."

Montalbano gave him a questioning look, and the youth felt obliged to add:

"I'm in my second year at the university, in philosophy. I want to become an epistemologist."

He seemed to have a clear idea of what he wanted, but he expressed it without the enthusiasm of the kids his age who'd already charted their course and wanted to follow it to the end.

But, if he remembered correctly, wasn't epistemology the philosophy of knowledge? What the hell did the philosophy of knowledge have to do with homicide?

"But why are you so interested in my methods of investigation, as you call them?"

"I'm sorry, I should have been more clear. I'm interested in the way your brain functions when you're conducting an investigation."

"Two plus two equals four."

"I'm sorry, I don't understand."

"That's a summary of how my brain functions."

For the first time, Harry Potter smiled.

"Would you be offended if I said I don't believe you?"

"Listen, I'm sorry to disappoint you, but I assure you—"

"I hope you don't mind if I insist. May I cite an example that directly concerns you?"

"Go ahead."

"Ingrid told me how the two of you met."

"And so?"

"For you, Ingrid should have represented the number four—that is, the sum of two plus two."

"I don't follow."

"She told me that she had been set up to appear like the prime suspect of a crime, or something like that, but that you, a police inspector, refused to lend credence to the evidence pointing to her guilt. Therefore in that case, you didn't believe that two plus two equaled four."

Smart kid, no doubt about that.

"Well, you see, in that case . . ."

"In that case, if I may, you realized at a certain point in the investigation that blindly following a rule of arithmetic would lead you astray. So you took another path. And that's what interests me. When and how this sort of deviation occurs in your mind. In short, how did your brain find the courage to abandon the solid ground of evidence and venture into the quicksands of hypothesis?"

"Sometimes I can't even explain it myself. But what, exactly, do you want from me?"

"I would like for you to allow me to follow you from up close. I promise you I won't be a bother. I wouldn't interfere in any way, believe me. I would only observe you in silence."

"I don't doubt that, but this is not a good time for it."

"Why do you say that?"

"Because at the moment, I haven't a single investigation ongoing. Tell you what: leave me a telephone number, and if anything interesting comes up, I'll let you know."

The look of childish disappointment that came over Arturo's face made the inspector feel sorry for him. He looked like a little boy who'd been denied some chocolate. The truth was that Montalbano really liked him. And it had been a while that he'd been feeling the need to talk to an intelligent person. So he wanted to give him a sort of consolation prize.

"Listen, it's true that something strange has been going on lately. But I should tell you straight off that it doesn't involve a crime or anything."

The kid looked like a starving dog who spots a bone with meat still attached to it.

"Anything's fine with me."

Montalbano pulled out of his pocket the three small sheets of paper with the poems about the treasure hunt, but not the other pages with his solutions. He told him what had happened so far, concluding:

"All right, these are the originals, which I want you to return to me. Solve one of the riddles on your own and then we can talk about it."

Arturo very nearly kissed his hands.

———

The next day at the station it seemed as if absolutely nothing was going to happen, as had been the case for over a month. From eight o'clock in the morning until one—that is, over a five-hour period—Catarella received only one phone call, but even that was from someone who wanted to know what he had to do to enter the police force.

At this point Montalbano, who'd been feeling very hungry since noon, realized he had a problem.

Doing nothing the whole blessed day, lolling about, sitting in the office reading a whole year's worth of Sunday supplements of the Milanese *Corriere della Sera* from 1920 that he'd bought from a street vendor, or staring fixedly at the wall in front of him in a state somewhere between yogic meditation and catatonia, plunged him into a sort of depressive melancholy. And so, as a way of warding off depression, his body instinctively began to feel a wolflike hunger that he was powerless to resist.

That very morning he'd had to loosen the belt on his trousers by a notch, a sign that his waist had grown disturbingly in circumference. The immediate upshot was that he'd quickly taken all his clothes off again, removed his plastic collar, slipped on a bathing suit and gone for an hour-long swim despite the fact that the water was so gelid he'd nearly had a heart attack.

At Enzo's trattoria, though he'd resolved to keep within reasonable limits of gluttony, he cut loose with a dish of swordfish *involtini* and ordered a second helping, even though he'd already scarfed down a broad variety of seafood antipasti and a heaping plate of *spaghetti alle vongole*.

A walk along the jetty therefore become a dire necessity, along with a little rest on the usual flat rock, accompanied by the requisite cigarette.

Around six o'clock the phone rang. It was Catarella.

"Chief, 'at't be 'at kid 'at came yisterday, the one sint by Signura Sciosciostrommi."

"Put him on."

"Chief, I can't put'im on 'cuz the subject in quession is onna premisses."

"Then show him in."

That way, he could chat with Arturo until it was time to go home.

"I didn't expect you back so soon," said Montalbano.

"Since I was in the area, I thought I'd try. Sorry I didn't call before coming."

"But do you live in Montelusa or—"

"No, I live in Vigàta. My parents live in Montelusa. I live alone in an apartment here in Vigàta. I like the sea."

Another point in the kid's favor.

"Have you had a chance to look at—"

"Yes, I've solved the riddles. Pretty basic stuff."

He took the pages out of his jacket pocket, laid them down on the desk, and continued.

"I didn't go to the Marinella Bar, which I assumed to be pointless, but to make up for it I did find the wooden shack up on the hill, at the end of Via dei Mille, and I even went inside."

"Did you notice the unusual wallpaper?"

Harry Potter smiled.

"Your challenger certainly seems to be creating a cult of personality around you."

"Are all the photos still up?"

"Yes, all of them. Why?"

"I dunno, just wondering. Got any ideas?"

"Yes."

"Let's hear them."

"Well, it's clear that your challenger wants things to appear a certain way. How shall I put it? He wants them to seem more innocent than they really are. In my opinion, the simplicity of the poetry, which you could even call stupidity, is intentional."

"You think so?"

"I'm quite convinced. There's a striking contrast between the disarming childishness of the little poems and the complex technological effort required to make those photos in the shack."

"Maybe there are two of them, one who writes the letters and the other—"

"I would rule that out."

"Why?"

"Because it looks in every way like a duel between two people, you and the other guy."

The kid reasoned well.

"And what kind of person do you think he is?"

"Well, so far we haven't got enough material to paint a complete portrait. All we can say is that he's a person who hides behind appearances—the rather harmless appearance of someone interested only in playing innocuous games."

"But in your opinion, that's not really the case."

"I really don't think so. There's something about all this that seems weird to me."

"So we're dealing, in short, with a cunning individual."

"More than just cunning: quite intelligent."

"Then all we can do is wait for the next letter," Montalbano concluded, standing up and holding out his hand.

"Will you keep me informed?"

"Of course. But tell me something. How did you manage to find Via dei Mille?"

"I got a map from city hall."

8

That evening, after waging a harsh battle with the four servings of *cuddriruni* he'd bought (he'd planned to eat only two, but lost the fight and ate them all), he phoned Livia. He decided not to tell her anything about the plastic collar.

"I've gained weight," he said dejectedly.

"That was all you needed."

Jesus, was Livia ever cranky sometimes! What did she mean by that? That he already had all the worst physical defects a man can have? Better pretend he didn't hear.

"I'm unable to control myself while eating—it must be because I've had nothing to do for the past month. I'm sure a clerk at the land registry office leads a more exciting life than I do."

"Are you telling me you've been twiddling your thumbs for the last month?"

Twiddling your thumbs! What an obnoxious expression! And when did anyone ever really twiddle their thumbs?

"Well, sort of."

"And you couldn't even find two days to come and see me?"

"No, you see, I thought about it, but then, maybe because I was hoping something would happen—"

"You were *hoping*? Hoping that something would go wrong to prevent you from coming? Nobody's forcing you, you know. You can sit there and do nothing for as long as you want for all I care! But don't start hoping I'm going to come down there!"

"Jesus, why don't you make a big deal out of it for a change! I used the wrong verb, okay? I meant to say *I was afraid* something would happen."

"I guess we *are* a bit verbally challenged, hm?"

"Well, *you* certainly aren't! Your command of the language is utterly flawless! You even use such elegant expressions as 'twiddling your thumbs'! Ha ha ha!"

The flare-up didn't last more than five minutes, after which the pitch began to descend, and soon they were both apologizing, and in the end Montalbano promised that the following day he would be on the six P.M. flight for Genoa.

The next morning, after he'd been in the office for about half an hour, the door opened with such a crash that Montalbano, who'd been following the progress of a fly along the edge of his desk with extreme concentration, jumped straight into the air.

"Beckin' yer partin', Chief, my foot slipped," said a mortified Catarella.

He'd had to knock with his foot because his hands were busy carrying a rather large parcel.

" 'Iss 'ere packitch was d'livvered juss now an' iss asposta be brung t'yiz poissonally in poisson."

"Says who?"

"Sez right 'ere onna packitch."

Montalbano bent down to read.

For Inspector Salvo Montalbano: Personal

"Who delivered it?"

"A li'l boy."

"Does it say what's in it?"

"Yessir, books."

He hadn't ordered any books either from the Vigàta bookstore or from any publishing house. Anyway, even if he had, they would've arrived through the mail, not been hand-delivered.

"Lemme see that," he said, getting up and going over to Catarella.

He grabbed the box and felt its weight. As big as it was, it should have held a good thirty books, if not more. And thirty books would have weighed much more than that parcel did.

The whole thing didn't add up.

"Put it on the coffee table."

The coffee table formed part of the sitting area in one corner of the office.

"C'n I open it?"

"Not now."

Catarella left and Montalbano went back to studying the fly, which was now exploring a sheet of paper with the letterhead of the Office of the Commissioner. But every so often his gaze fell on the parcel. He was dying of curiosity.

At a certain point he couldn't stand it any longer, so he got up and went and sat in one of the armchairs to get a better look at it.

It was slightly rectangular, about a foot and a half high, wrapped in normal packing paper, and cross-tied with heavy string.

Why should this most common of parcels disturb him so?

Well, there was no return address, it had been hand-delivered by an unidentifiable little boy, it claimed to contain books he'd never ordered, and, finally, that specification, *Personal*, was something you normally found on letters, not on packages. All these things were rather unusual.

And there was another thing, too. . . . Ah, yes, as if it had been scripted, the previous evening he'd heard on TV that an anarchist group had sent a package of explosives to a carabinieri station.

There weren't any anarchists in Vigàta, but there were plenty of assholes.

He'd better go about this with caution, but without asking anyone's help.

He took the parcel in both hands and squeezed it hard. He heard a strange, muffled sound a little like a click, which made him bolt to his feet and take cover behind the desk, waiting for an explosion that never came.

What came instead was Mimì Augello. How was it possible the guy always showed up when he wasn't supposed to?

"Which movie is it this time?" he inquired. "*The Haunted House? Nightmare on Elm Street? Montalbano Versus the Ghosts?*"

"Mimì, get out of here and stop bugging me," said the inspector, standing up and giving him the sort of look that made him understand that it was better to do as he said without any arguments.

"All right, but it might not be a bad idea to have yourself looked at by a doctor sometime," he said, leaving.

Montalbano went and locked the door, then got back down to work.

He sat down again in the armchair, leaned all the way forward until his head was a few millimeters from the parcel, brought his hands to either side, squeezed hard, and heard the same click.

This time, however, he didn't run for cover. He didn't even move, because he finally understood what it was.

There had to be a tin box wrapped up inside the package. He removed the packing paper carefully, trying to move the parcel as little as possible.

He'd guessed right.

It was an old box of Fratelli Lazzaroni biscotti.

He remembered that when he was a boy his auntie had one exactly like it, in which she kept letters and photographs.

This one was even older and must have dated from before the War. In fact, on the lid, which displayed the medals and prizes won in biscotti competitions, there was also the proud inscription: *By Appointment to H.M. the King.*

The lid was held in place by several rounds of adhesive tape. The inspector grabbed the box, lifted it with both hands, brought it to his ear, and shook it lightly. He couldn't hear anything moving around inside.

So he got up, grabbed a pair of scissors, and removed all the tape.

Now came the hard part: lifting the lid. If it was a bomb, that would certainly be the act that triggered the explosion.

But how strong would the eventual explosion be? It was possible that, aside from him, it would kill a few others and bring half the building down.

Wouldn't it be better to call the bomb squad? But then if it turned out there really were only biscotti or some other kind of cookie inside, wouldn't he end up looking ridiculous?

The only solution was to go it alone and take the chance.

He was sweating. Removing his jacket, he knelt down in front of the low table, took the box in his hands, and with his thumbs pressed the lid up by half a millimeter, to see if he could look inside.

Despite the tension, he started laughing and forgot everything for a moment.

He'd remembered a game show he'd happened to watch a few times on TV, where the host would open packages using the same technique.

Wiping the sweat from his brow with his arm, he started again from the beginning. It took him a good five minutes to raise the lid, which he then set down on the floor. Inside was a bundle of oilcloth, inserted in a little bag of transparent nylon.

Taking the scissors, he cut off the whole top of the nylon bag without ever taking the bundle out of the box. At this point he could have picked up the oilcloth and unwrapped it, but he decided he would rather cut off the top with the scissors. It wasn't an easy task, but some ten minutes later the bundle was practically open, thanks to a few cuts. All he would have to do was reach in, grip the oilcloth, and lift it. Setting the scissors down, he pinched the two ends of the cloth with his fingers and pulled it outwards.

He saw two dead eyes staring up at him. When the sickly sweet smell of blood rose to his nostrils, he leapt to his feet, gave a loud cry, went and crashed into the door, unlocked it, and found Mimì Augello standing in front of him.

"What happened?"

"There's . . . it looks like a head inside the package."

Meanwhile Fazio had arrived.

"I heard a yell. . . . What happened?"

"Come with me," Augello said to him.

They went into the office. Montalbano heaved a long sigh and followed them. Augello had already entirely unwrapped the cloth.

"It's a lamb's head," he said.

Sticking a hand into the parcel, he pulled out, by one

corner, an envelope wrapped in bloodstained nylon, then bent his head forward to read through the transparent fabric.

"It's addressed to you, Salvo," he said. "It says: *Treasure Hunt*."

As Mimì set the letter down on the desk, Montalbano, looking a little pale, went and locked the door again.

"Nobody, aside from you two, is to know anything about this, is that clear?" he said to Mimì and Fazio.

"This is a typical Mafia-style intimidation tactic that definitely should not be hushed up," Augello retorted. "And I don't intend—"

"Mimì, save the highfalutin speech, 'cause the Mafia doesn't have a goddamn thing to do with this."

"So what's it about, then?"

"It's about a treasure hunt. Isn't that what the envelope says?"

"Listen," Mimì said coldly, "either you tell me straightaway what this is really about, or I'm going to walk out of this room and after that I don't want to hear another word about it."

"Mimì, I can't tell you what it's about because it's so absurd that—"

"As you wish," Mimì said resentfully.

He turned the key, opened the door, and left.

"Go and get two pairs of latex gloves, some plastic bags, and then come back," Montalbano said to Fazio.

He sat down at his desk and looked at the envelope. As far as one could tell through the stained nylon, neither the envelope nor the handwriting was any different from the prior specimens.

Fazio returned.

"Lock the door."

Fazio handed him a pair of gloves and then put on his own.

"What do you want me to do?" he asked.

"Take the head out. But put everything else in the plastic bags: the oilcloth, the box itself, and so on. We'll try to get some fingerprints from them."

"Can I ask a question, Chief?"

"Sure, what is it?"

"What do you want fingerprints for? Cutting off a lamb's head isn't the kind of thing you find listed in the penal code."

He'd said it in Italian, as if to distance the question, make it less personal. Fazio was being as cautious as Mimì had just been rash.

"I don't know what to tell you. I have a sort of premonition that we may need them in the future."

The inspector put his gloves on and picked up the envelope. The sheet of nylon wrapped around it was held in place by two pieces of tape. Removing these, he unwound the sheet and freed the envelope. Then he put the sheet of nylon and two pieces of tape in one of the plastic bags Fazio had brought.

He then opened the envelope with a letter opener, pulled out the usual half-sheet of paper, and put this into his jacket pocket. Since the page was folded in two, he couldn't see what was written on it.

"All done," said Fazio.

Montalbano stood up and went over to him.

Fazio had set the lamb's head down on the floor on a sheet of newspaper. The oilcloth and tin box were already in two separate plastic bags.

"What should I do with the head?"

"Go and throw it away in a garbage bin, but don't let anyone see you."

"All right."

"Did you have a look at it? What do you think?"

"Well, first the lamb was killed—maybe strangled with a rope—and then whoever killed it tried to cut its head off. But since he wasn't a butcher and had no experience at that sort of thing, it looks like he tried first with a knife and then used a power saw. You can tell by the clean cut of the bone."

"And when was it done, would you say?"

"Last night. The meat is still fresh. Before putting the head in the oilcloth, they let it drain for a while so that there wouldn't be too much blood in the box."

"Is there still room in that closet in your office?"

"Yes."

"Have you got a key for it?"

"Yes."

"Go and put the head in your closet, then come back, take the evidence, including the bag on my desk, put it all in the closet, then lock it. And keep the key with you."

He opened the half-sheet only once, read it—another poem—grabbed a piece of paper, copied the poem, put the half-sheet in the plastic bag and sealed it. Then he folded the sheet of paper with the copied poem on it and put this in his pocket.

The treasure hunt had taken a curious turn.

According to what Fazio had told him—and he had no reason to doubt him—the prankster had not gone to a butcher's to buy a lamb's head, but had done everything himself, with his own two hands.

Which suggested a few interesting things.

The first was that the person in question had been cold-blooded and determined enough to get a living lamb, strangle it with a rope, and then saw off its head, all for the sole purpose of continuing a sort of game.

Who among them, on the police force, starting with him, Montalbano, would have been able to do such a thing? Nobody, he could bet the house on it. And someone like that, who thought that way, who acted that way—could he be a potential murderer?

The second thing was that the person must necessarily have a country property with a few animals on it, even if he normally lived in town. He surely hadn't gone and stolen the lamb. Too risky. A property in the countryside nearby, where he also kept a power saw to cut tree branches.

Whatever the case, it was clear that the game was getting out of hand.

Which led him to the conclusion that it was no longer

advisable to leave Vigàta to spend a few days in Boccadasse with Livia.

O matre santa! He and Livia had arranged for her to come and get him at the airport!

It was better to let her know at once, while she was still at the office, especially as this would prevent her from making a scene, since she'd be surrounded by her colleagues. He dialed the direct number and Livia herself picked up. He spoke in a single stream of words, a single breath, not giving Livia the time to cut in.

"Listen, Livia, the hitch that I was ho— er, fearing would come up has suddenly just now materialized and I really don't think I can leave. You've got to believe me, I feel terribly mortified, especially because I really wanted to come, really . . . Hello? Hello?"

But Livia had already hung up. Well, never mind. When they talked that evening he would have to put up with everything she had to say, and he really couldn't blame her.

This time at Enzo's he didn't pig out. He ate a normal meal, but took a walk out to the lighthouse just the same.

Sitting down on the flat rock, he fired up a cigarette, and not until he'd finished it did he take the piece of paper with the poem out of his pocket.

The head of the sheep
is the tastiest treat.

It's a part you must keep
and will most want to eat.

Stewing is one way to make it,
though roasting is also good,
and some say you should bake it:
either way it's great food!

Once you've had a thorough taste,
drink two glasses of wine
and proceed without haste
to a place where you'll find

a small piece of the sky.
Here you should linger awhile.
No scales will fall from your eye,
no answer will make you smile.

At first glance, he didn't understand where his challenger was trying to go with this. So he reread the poem from the beginning. And he became convinced that it was again directing him to a place, but also kindly warning him that, once he got there, he wouldn't find anything. But if, upon reaching the end, he wasn't going to receive any new instructions for getting to the next stage, what point was there in having him find the way? None. Maybe the present stage of the treasure hunt was a moment of rest? No, it didn't make sense. He decided to ignore it, or at least take his time. He wouldn't go out searching right away. But then he reconsidered. It was possible that even if his challenger wasn't giving any direct instructions, he himself, once there, might nevertheless find something of use to him. He had an idea. He raced back to his car, and drove off with the second stanza in his head, the one that began, *Stewing is one way to make it . . .*

The rolling metal shutter of Enzo's trattoria was pulled three-quarters down. Which meant that there was someone inside. He parked, got out, went up to the shutter and squatted.

"Anybody there?"

"Who is it?"

"Montalbano."

"Wait, I'll come and open."

When Enzo saw the inspector standing before him, he gave him a puzzled look.

"What is it, Inspector?"

"I need some information. How many restaurants and trattorias are there in Vigàta?"

"Just a second while I count."

He closed his eyes and started counting with his fingers.

"Eleven, I think," he finally said.

"Are there any that serve lamb's head?"

Enzo opened his eyes wide in astonishment.

"You feel like eating lamb's head?"

"It's the furthest thing from my mind. I just want to know."

"No trattoria or restaurant around here makes it, Inspector. Maybe if you order it specially. But as a regular dish, not a chance."

He paused.

"But I think I remember somebody saying, a while back, that there was a place where . . ."

He seemed doubtful, and Montalbano didn't force him.

"Let's go inside," Enzo said finally. "Would you like a coffee?"

"Sure, why not?"

There was a waiter mopping the floor. Enzo went and busied himself in the kitchen, then returned a few minutes later. The coffee was good, but Enzo still seemed lost in thought. All at once he slapped his forehead.

"Michele Lauria!"

He ran over to the wall phone, grabbed the phone book that was on a wooden shelf beside it, flipped a few pages, and found a number.

"Michè, is this an okay time to call? Can you talk for a minute? I wanted to ask you something. Was it you that mentioned a wine tavern to me where they also sell roast meats? Including lamb's head? Yes? And can you tell me where it is and how you get there?"

He listened for a few moments, thanked him, set down the receiver, and turned towards Montalbano with a big smile.

"Do you know the road to Gallotta?"

9

And so he was back on the hamster wheel. Montalbano took the roundabout, began to drive up Via dei Mille, passed the cemetery, the ugly buildings, the little houses, and reached the top, the end of the road. He stopped for a moment. On the left, the wooden shack with the photographs. Gallotta straight ahead, about four miles away. In between lay the road that plunged into the valley and climbed back up the hill, around the top of which the town sat perched. Those four miles of road cutting through the countryside were unpaved, a dirt road, though practicable for cars. He'd driven down it once before, over the course of an investigation, and remembered it well.

He restarted the car and started to descend slowly into the valley. After a couple of miles the climb began. Up to that point he had crossed paths with one other car coming the other way and three men on horseback.

He kept looking to the left and right for signs, but saw nothing. At last, when he was starting to lose hope, about a quarter mile from Gallotta, on the left, he saw a dirt lane marked by a tree with a piece of wooden plank nailed to it bearing the words: WINE AND FOODE.

The lane was narrow, but the car could fit. It was lined on both sides with a dense growth of tall trees. About thirty yards up there was a clearing with a small two-story house. On the front door there was the same sign as on the tree, with the same spelling mistake, except that the letters were all larger. Sitting beside the door in a wicker chair was a disheveled woman of about seventy wearing an apron and slippers.

When she saw a car coming, she stood up and went inside. The inspector pulled up, got out of the car, and followed her. Inside was a large room with some ten tables covered with oilcloth and a counter at the back, which the woman had gone behind. Behind her were two barrels of wine, a rather large refrigerator, and built-in shelves with bottles and glasses.

"What can I get for you?"

"A glass of wine, thanks."

The woman tapped it directly from the barrel. It was excellent.

"What sort of food have you got?"

"That's only in the evening, when we make stuff to eat with the wine."

So they only cooked in the evenings, when the townfolk came to play cards and drink.

"Is it true that you make lamb's head?"

"Yessir, but only Saturdays. When there's more people."

"How do you cook it?"

"Sometimes we stew it, sometimes we fry it, or roast it, or bake it . . ."

It all corresponded.

"What about the other days?"

"Sausages, pork ribs, *cacio all'argintera*, that kind of thing."

"Could I have another?"

The old woman poured him another glass. He paid, said goodbye, and went out. Now, what came next? He took the poem out of his pocket.

> *. . . drink two glasses of wine*
> *and proceed without haste*
> *to a place where you'll find*
>
> *a small piece of the sky.*

Now came the hard part. The poem's instructions were too vague. *Proceed without haste.* Fine, but where to? Get in the car and . . . No, wait a second. He sensed instinctively that he shouldn't take the car.

And indirectly, the poem itself implied this. Eat the sheep's head, drink two glasses of wine, proceed without haste—that is, take a nice slow walk, to aid digestion, the way he customarily did along the jetty after eating. Therefore the place that looked like a piece of the sky must be somewhere around there. He took a good look around. And he noticed that the dirt track he had taken to the clearing in which he now stood continued. Except that it stopped being a dirt road and turned into a sort of trail through the dense growth of trees, full of pits and dips. He drew near to it.

There were visible tire tracks from cars, clearly off-road vehicles. His car could never manage it. Indeed, probably no town car could.

The woman came out and sat back down in the wicker chair.

He could have asked her where the path led, but he didn't want to attract too much attention to himself, which might spark curiosity and questions. The best thing was to find out for himself.

He realized immediately, after taking his first steps, that even on foot it wasn't going to be easy. On either side of the trail were old, huge carob trees, which cast dark shadows and had roots that crisscrossed the path here and there like snakes under sand. It was an unending alternation of humps and dips that forced you to balance your body in a precarious way. If you twisted an ankle, you were screwed. Days would go by before anyone found you. A hare darted hastily across the path in front of him. Then a grass snake over six feet long, a big green thing that didn't deem him worthy of a glance. How long had it been since he'd seen animals running free? And how long since he'd heard so many birds all singing together?

After some ten minutes of this, he began to feel tired. He wasn't used to walking with one foot a yard higher than the other, with his body leaning worse than the Tower of Pisa. He sat down under a carob tree and fired up a cigarette.

When he was a little kid, he was told that quadrupeds liked to eat carob beans, but he really liked them himself, though he wasn't a quadruped. He gobbled them up raw, when they were really sweet, as well as baked, when they took on a slightly bitterish taste. One time he ate so many that he had a bellyache for two days.

Feeling sufficiently rested, he resumed walking. Some ten minutes later he realized he'd reached his destination. The path led to a very large clearing with a tiny little lake in the middle. It wasn't clear how it had formed or what it was doing there. It was about as big as a soccer field, perfectly circular, and looked like an artificial lake but wasn't. His challenger had been correct in writing that it was a small piece of the sky. Because the motionless water had the exact same color as the sky. A flock of birds were quenching their thirst and a few were also bathing. A short distance away from them, on the shore, a curled-up dog lay asleep.

Montalbano sat down on the ground.

The path circled the little lake, then climbed up a slope as far as a small two-story house, behind which was a sort of thicket. The inspector figured that if he'd come this far, he might as well forge on.

After another brief rest, he stood up and headed towards the house.

As he slowly approached and began to get a better look at it, he noticed that the house was half in ruins. The front door was gone, as was the frame of the window next to it. And the window of the floor above was likewise simply a rectangular opening.

He went inside.

The ground floor consisted of a single room. To the right were the remains of a brickwork stove with two wood-fired burners. To one side, a sort of stone sink built into the wall and the remains of a clay jug beside it. On the floor, a few condoms, two syringes, and a sleeping bag riddled with holes . . .

No furniture.

To the left, a wooden staircase led upstairs. Before climbing it, Montalbano shook it with both hands to see if it would hold up. The wood was neither damp nor worm-eaten. He went up.

The upstairs room was totally empty, like the one below. Here, too, condoms and syringes.

He raced out of the house, afraid that if he lingered there too long, he might find fleas running all over his body.

He sat for a while eyeing the lake. Charming, no doubt, but it told him nothing at all that might relate to the treasure hunt. After all, his challenger had frankly warned him:

No scales will fall from your eye,
no answer will make you smile.

He couldn't claim to have wasted his time, because his walk had been quite pleasant and healthy. Or, perhaps not so healthy as all that, since a flea had just bitten him on the hand.

———

Going back the same way he had come, still leaning like the Tower of Pisa as he walked, medical collar pinching his neck because he was sweating so profusely, he got very tired.

So tired that when he reached the clearing where he'd left the car, he got inside and just rested for a few minutes, smoking a cigarette. The wicker chair beside the door was empty. Perhaps the old woman had gone inside to prepare the food for that evening.

A short while later, he started up the car and drove off.

The only result he'd obtained—he thought while driving back to headquarters—was no big deal, but it was a little hole in the darkness around him, no bigger than the head of a pin, through which shone a faint shaft of light.

And this was that Via dei Mille, the road to Gallotta, and the area around Gallotta itself, was well-known and well-traveled terrain for the prankster. Montalbano was more than certain that not even Fazio knew about the little lake the color of the sky.

"Anyone call for me, Cat?"

"Nossir, Chief, not f'yiz or fr'innybuddy ellis."

So the dead calm continued. As he was about to head back to his office, Catarella stopped him.

"Chief, tink y'could gimme a hand?"

"With what?"

"Witta crassword puzzle."

"What do you want to know?"

"'Ere iss writt' 'at 'they fought against the mice.' Five litters. Mine comes out 'bread.' But I never seen bread fightin' wit' mice. If anyting, iss the mice eatin' the bread."

"It's the 'Batracomiomachia,'" said the inspector.

Catarella turned pale.

"*Matre santa*, Chief, wha' kinda words come outta you mout'!"

"Don't worry, the word you're looking for is 'frogs.'"

"'Scuse me, Chief, but then wha'ss the 'thing that sees at night,' ain't it a bat?"

"No, Cat, it's radar."

"Jeezis, iss true! Tanks, Chief!"

"Listen, Cat, do you know that little lake up by Gallotta?"

"Nossir, Chief, when I go onna nickpick, I like to go to the beach."

"Get Fazio for me, would you?"

How was it that his desk was newly covered with papers to sign? It occurred to him that if all of mankind suddenly vanished from the face of the earth, for days and days the papers to be signed would probably keep on mysteriously accumulating on the desks of the world's offices.

"What is it, Chief?"

"Fazio, do you know anything about a very small lake in the area outside Gallotta?"

"Yeah, sure."

Fazio's answer took him by surprise. He'd been totally convinced that even Fazio didn't know about it.

"Do you go there for nickpicks, as Catarella calls them?"

"Nah, Chief, I'm not too keen on picnics, but about two years before you came here to work, something happened there."

"What kind of thing?"

"Near the lake there's a little house where a peasant used to live, a widower, I think his name was Parisi—yeah, Tano Parisi, who lived with a beautiful daughter, sixteen years old. One day Tano came and reported the disappearance of his daughter, whose name I don't remember. And she's never been heard from since."

"Was there an investigation?"

"Of course! I took part in it myself. The chief inspector at the time, Bonvicino, had the father arrested."

"Why?"

"There were rumors that Tano, the father, took advantage of her. The town doctor didn't say it outright, but he let Inspector Bonvicino know that the girl was pregnant."

"But couldn't she have had a relationship with somebody else?"

"Well, exactly. Other folks in town said that it was true that the father took advantage of her, but that she was also doing it with a man in Gallotta. They said he was the one that got the kid pregnant, and that the girl jumped in the lake and killed herself because she was too scared to tell her father she was pregnant."

"But is it deep enough?"

"It's extremely deep, Chief. Every so often some geologist goes up there to study it. They have no explanation for it."

"Doesn't it have a name?"

"You mean the lake?"

"Yes."

"They just call it *'u Lacu d'o Signuri*, God's Lake. They say that God, when he stretched the canvas of the sky over creation, had a little piece left over. So he tore it off, rolled it up, poked his finger into the ground to make a really deep hole, right there outside Gallotta, stuck the rolled-up sky all the way down and then changed it to water. And that's why it's so deep and has that color."

So his challenger also knew the legend.

"And what ever happened to the girl's father?"

"He was acquitted for lack of evidence. But the people who kept on believing he was his own daughter's killer wouldn't give up and on certain nights they'd go and shoot at his house. Tano figured that sooner or later they were going to kill him, so he moved to another town. But why are you so interested in this lake? Did something happen at the campsite?"

"What campsite?"

"For a while some foreign kids've been camping in the woods behind the house. Livin' the natural life, bare-assed and drugged out. Every so often things take a bad turn and somebody gets knifed."

"Chief? 'At'd be your cleanin' lady onna line. C'n I put her true?"

"Go ahead . . . Hello, Adelì. How are you feeling?"

"Fine, sir. I wannit a say I's comin' a beck a work tomorrow."

"Do you feel up to it?"

"Yessir, I do. But you gotta do me a favor. I don' wanna looka like I's a stick a my nose inna you business . . ."

"Go on, speak."

"You gotta get ridda those dolls. They gimme the creeps. Jesus, whatta scare they givva me!"

"Don't worry, Adelì, they're already gone."

He ate very little. He didn't like eating in restaurants alone at night. By now he was accustomed to eating at home in the evening. At least it would be the last time, and tomorrow he could open the refrigerator or oven and find another of Adelina's wonderful surprises.

He sat at home watching the late edition of the news, national and local. In Salemi a man returning from his nearby country house was murdered and, naturally, nobody had heard or seen a thing. The motive appeared to have been a matter of inheritance that had been dragging on for years, but the case was turning out to be rather complicated just the same. Montalbano suddenly felt a pang of envy for the police detective in charge of the investigation.

What? Was he starting to suffer from homicide withdrawal? Before going to bed, he decided to try to make peace with Livia, and so he called her.

"Hi. Listen, despite the fact that you hung up on me this morning—"

"I didn't hang up on you."

"You didn't?"

"No, I didn't. The line went dead. I kept saying 'hello, hello' and then I finally hung up."

"Why didn't you try calling back?"

"Because I'd already heard the essential part, that is, that you weren't coming anymore, and I didn't feel like phoning you from the office. And if you really want to know, I knew all along you wouldn't come."

"Livia, I swear—"

"Just drop it."

There was a pause, with the estimated temperature at about 40 below. Then Livia resumed talking, though it probably would have been better if she hadn't.

"And what's the excuse this time?"

"Excuse me, but what excuse are you talking about?"

"The one you've fabricated so you won't have to come."

"There is no excuse! I don't need to fabricate excuses for myself, you know! What happened is this: in spite of myself, I've become involved in a treasure hunt and have to—"

135

"You whaaaa . . . ?!"

Matre santa, he'd made a big mistake, beginning his argument that way! How was he going to clear things up now? He would never manage, not in a million years! All the same, he had nothing left to lose, so he might as well try.

"Just listen to me for a moment, please. I can explain."

"What on earth is there to explain? A treasure hunt? I know how they work, I've gone on a few myself, in my time."

"No, no, this one's a little different, because—"

"And who's your partner? Ingrid, or someone I haven't yet had the pleasure of meeting?"

"Come on, what has Ingr—"

"Just stop it! That's enough! Our little man isn't coming to see me because he has to take part in a treasure hunt with his little girlfriend! You know what I say? I'm sick and tired of this! Really and truly!"

"You think I'm not?"

Livia hung up. And a good thing too, because hearing himself called "little man," Montalbano had lost the light of reason.

To conclude, instead of making peace, he had simply aggravated the damage already done. But when you came right down to it, it wasn't entirely his fault. Livia never let him finish what he was saying, always interrupting him, and he always ended up getting upset.

At any rate, it was probably best not to call her back, at least not that evening.

The following morning he headed straight for Montelusa Hospital.

They examined him and said he no longer needed to wear the collar.

He felt the way a slave freed of his chains must have felt.

"Any news, any phone calls?"

"Nuttin', Chief. Couldja gimme a hand?"

"What are you doing?"

"A rebus."

"I'm not any good at those."

It wasn't true, but how could a police inspector with a brilliant past, no matter how dull his present, stoop to solving puzzles for a switchboard operator who, on top of everything, was Catarella?

Then, sometime past eleven, after he'd been signing papers for over two hours, a call from Arturo came in.

"Any new developments, Inspector?"

"Well, yes."

"Feel like talking about it?"

"Over the phone? Not really. It would take too long."

"Can I drop by, then?"

He didn't feel much like thinking that morning. Apparently the fact of applying useless signatures to even more useless sheets of paper paralyzed his brain.

"Could you come around five o'clock?"

"Sure, why not? See you at five then. I'll be right on time."

The kid was dying to know the latest developments, you could tell from his voice.

After stuffing himself with pasta in squid ink and a good pound of jumbo shrimp, he took his customary walk out to the lighthouse, sat down on the flat rock, and spent a good half hour busting the balls of a crab.

He then returned to the office. Arturo showed up at five on the dot.

At that moment Montalbano was busy talking on the phone with the chief of the commissioner's cabinet, Dr. Lattes, who wanted to know why nobody in the inspector's office had replied yet to questionnaire no. 3289/PA/045, a document which Montalbano didn't know the first thing about or where it might be.

"I'll get on it right away, Doctor."

He hung up and rang Fazio.

"Could you come in for a second?"

While waiting, he wrote down the number of the questionnaire on a sheet of paper. Fazio arrived.

"Listen, they want an immediate reply to the questionnaire with this reference number. Which means . . ." he said, handing him the paper, "take all the papers here on the desk into your office and see if you can't find it."

It took Fazio two trips to clear off Montalbano's desk.

10

The whole time he'd been waiting, Arturo had fidgeted restlessly in his chair. Once Fazio finished, he couldn't hold himself back any longer.

"So," he said impatiently.

Without a word Montalbano pulled the letter with the poem out of his pocket and handed it to him. The kid practically snatched it out of his hand.

"It's obviously about another path for you to follow," he said after reading it twice.

Montalbano decided to put him to the test. He wanted to see just how intelligent the kid was.

"Fine, but do you know where? I, frankly, can't make any sense of it this time. To the point that I haven't even tried to find it like last time. For example, what's this business about a sheep's head?"

"Well, in my opinion, and I could be wrong, the main point is to find a place, or an establishment, where they regularly cook lamb's head."

"You think so? You mean a restaurant in Vigàta?"

"I don't think you normally find that sort of dish in a restaurant. Maybe a tavern of some sort."

"And then what? Once you find the place, in what direction are you supposed to 'proceed without haste'? It doesn't say."

"Probably once you figure out where the place is, you'll know what direction to go in."

"I suppose you're right, but the whole search seems pointless, a waste of time and effort."

"Why?"

"Didn't you read the last two lines? It says there will be no answers to my questions. So why waste my time?"

"I don't think that's really what they mean."

"Then what do they mean, in your opinion?"

"I think your adversary is trying to say that since you won't find any new instructions from him there, you'll have to discover, with your intuition, something that might later prove useful to you."

"You may very well be right, but I have no intention anymore of doing anything. I refuse to continue playing this stupid game."

An expression of disappointment came over the young man's face. The boy's face, actually. Because he really did seem like a little boy at that moment.

"You're giving up?!"

Was he going to start crying?

"I'm afraid so."

"But you can't back out now!"

"And why not? It certainly wasn't my idea to play this game, and nobody even asked me if I wanted to play. So I can withdraw whenever I feel like it."

"Can I make a suggestion?" Arturo asked.

He was folding his hands as if in prayer. Montalbano's threat to stop playing the game had put him in a state of agitation.

"Go ahead."

"What if I went in your place?"

"I don't think that's such a good idea."

"Why not?"

"If my adversary discovers you're helping me . . ."

"But I'll make sure I'm not discovered! I'll be very careful!"

"Do you really think you can?"

"Try me."

That was what Montalbano was hoping he would say. He fell silent for a few moments, as though weighing the pros and cons of the proposal, and then said:

"All right."

Arturo leapt to his feet, eyes aglitter with joy.

"Thank you for having faith in me. I'll be back in touch soon."

They shook hands. The youth left in a big hurry. He was like a dog pursuing a hare.

Five minutes later, Fazio came in.

"Found it!"

To fill out questionnaire no. 3289/PA/045, "pertaining to perspectives and aspects of the duties and functions of the office of Director of the Archives," it took him well over an hour, between curses, expletives, and moments of dejection so dark as to push him to the brink of suicide.

Before leaving the station, he thought he should phone Ingrid. He wanted to ask her a few things about young Arturo, whom he felt rather perplexed about. Though he was unlikely to find her at home at that hour, since she would surely be out with some girlfriend or boyfriend, he decided to try just the same.

"Hullo, hullo, hoodare?" asked a basso profondo voice, rather like that of a blues singer or someone from the Bolshoi men's choir, take your pick, except that it belonged to a woman.

Ingrid's specialty was changing housekeepers and manservants about every two weeks, only because she was rather fickle about them, but she always picked people from places so obscure that to find them on a map you needed an enormous magnifying glass.

"Montalbano here."

"Wich you name? Montabbano or Heer?"

What an idea, calling oneself Heer! Herr Heer here! He really thought he would like that. The inspector replied in the same language.

"Montabbano. Wan talk to Signora Ingrid."

"Wett."

Of course he would wait. And wait he did, for a good five minutes over the course of which he said "Hello, hello" quite a few times, in the terror that the line had gone dead and that he would have to start all over again by talking to that housekeeper from Upper Turkistan.

"Ciao, Salvo. What a lovely surprise!"

"Where's your new housekeeper from?"

"I don't know, but tomorrow they're sending me another one."

Damn, just when he was starting to learn the language.

"What are you doing this evening?"

"I see you don't waste any time getting to the point. I'm busy. I have a date with a friend who's got almost the same name as you, Montabbano. But I can't join him for another hour or so."

"I didn't dare hope."

She chuckled.

"These are lean times, Salvo."

"You're telling me! All right, then. I'll wait for you in Marinella, then we can decide where to go."

On his way out he was stopped by Catarella.

"Whassup, Chief, you leavin'? C'n ya gimme a li'l hand?"

"All right, go ahead."

"Tanks, Chief."

"Rebus or crossword?"

"Crasswoid."

"Go ahead."

"A mouth full of gold. Wassatt? Summon 'oo wenna the dennist winn 'ey yousta give yiz gole teet? My Uncle Giuvanni, wenn 'e got back from Amurca, 'e 'ad two gole teet."

"No, Cat. It's the dawn that has a mouth full of gold."

"Jeezis, Chief, you're good! A genus! Jess like Lionardo!"

He didn't dare ask Catarella if he was referring to Leonardo da Vinci.

Maybe Adelina had had the bright idea to celebrate her return in grand fashion.

And indeed, when he opened the refrigerator before anything else, he saw before him some ten *involtini* of swordfish made just the way he liked them and two large bulbs of fennel cut and cleaned, just the thing for refreshing the palate. And there was even a bottle of chilled wine. On the inside part of the door was also a sheet of paper with the words: *Look in oven too*. And so he looked.

In the oven he found a casserole of *pasta 'ncasciata*.

Not even by force or seduction would Ingrid ever be able to persuade him to go and eat in some restaurant. Weighing the pros and cons, he grabbed another bottle of white and put it in the fridge. And at that exact moment he remembered he didn't have a drop of whisky in the house.

He went out again, leaving the door ajar and the light on in the entrance hall, got in the car and went to the Marinella Bar, where they made him pay double for whisky.

Should he buy one or two bottles? Better stick with one, not to economize or anything, but because if they should drink more than one, Ingrid would be in no condition to drive home to Montelusa. Which meant a rough night for him.

Pulling back in at home, it looked as if Ingrid had already arrived, to judge from the missile in front of the house.

He went in. Ingrid had opened the French door and was setting the table on the veranda. On the table were already two bottles of whisky she had brought with her.

"Since we drank it all the other night . . ." she said.

He'd tried to prevent it but hadn't succeeded. Tonight would surely be a replay of last time.

"Maybe you would have rather gone to a restaurant?" he said.

"I wouldn't dream of it, not after I saw what Adelina made for you."

Smart woman and a true friend, no doubt about it.

"I peeked under the bed and noticed that the dolls were gone," Ingrid continued with a smirk. "Where are they going to pop up tonight?"

"Nowhere. I took them to the police station."

"For your men to enjoy like the spoils of war?"

"I really don't think they need any surrogates."

"Have you ever found out why there was that . . . that duplication?"

"No. But I have a strange feeling that it didn't end there. I'm going into the kitchen to light the oven."

She followed him.

"Oh, listen . . . ," she said moments later. "I don't know whether . . ."

She stopped, clearly hesitating.

"What is it?"

"I think I did something stupid a few minutes ago."

"Tell me."

"Just as I was coming in, I heard the phone ringing and so I picked up. I did it automatically, without thinking, I'm so sorry."

"Come on! Who was it?"

"Livia."

Shit!

Seeing Montalbano's face, she tried to control the damage.

"Or at least I thought it was her."

Why had she called at an off-hour? Maybe she needed to tell him something important?

"What did she say?"

"After I said hello, she asked me something like, 'How's the treasure hunt going?' And then she immediately hung up. But I'm not sure I understood correctly."

"You understood perfectly."

Alas. What to do now? Call her back? But Livia, knowing Ingrid was there with him, was liable not to answer or, if she did answer, to kick up such a row that she would turn his stomach to mush. Better not do anything for the moment, take no initiatives. If he talked to Livia now, he would likely have trouble digesting the *pasta 'ncasciata* and *involtini*.

When they were done they cleared the table, then went and sat back down on the veranda with a bottle and two glasses.

The night seemed under its own spell: there wasn't a breath of wind, the stars sparkled crisply in the sky, and the sea was completely still.

"We women are a curious lot," Ingrid began. "And for the duration of this wonderful dinner I've been unable to get Livia's words out of my head."

"Better not . . ."

But Ingrid insisted.

"Don't you want to tell me what she meant by 'treasure hunt'? I really didn't know you liked those kinds of games. Not to mention that when I repeated what she said, you made such a face!"

"Well, you see, it's not a real treasure hunt . . . In reality I'm involved in a sort of challenge which some unknown person calls a treasure hunt."

"Why do you call it a challenge?"

"Because he's the one organizing the game, and I'm his only competition. Maybe it'd be better to call it a duel. At least until the other day."

"Why, what happened the other day?"

"I met your friend Arturo."

"Ah, I'd forgotten about that! What did you make of him?"

"He seems like a very smart kid. And a little complicated, I'd say. He wants to find out how my brain works during an investigation. Imagine that! It seemed to me like a ridiculous proposition from the very start."

"So did you tell him no?"

"I wanted to, but then I let myself be talked into it—not so much by his words but by his obvious enthusiasm. So I decided to let him in on the secret challenge, and he immediately lit up like a match. I even sent him on the treasure hunt in my place."

"Really! He must be so happy! He so admires you!"

"How did you meet him?"

"Through Carlo, his father, who'd been a friend of my husband's at the university and a fellow traveler in his political adventures."

"Were you—"

"Before you finish your question, I can tell you there's never been anything between the two of us. My husband invited him to lunch not long after I'd first come to live in Montelusa, and that was when I met Arturo, who was a little boy at the time. And the spitting image of Harry Potter. Whom he still resembles."

"What's his mother like?"

"His mother died while giving birth to him. He was more or less raised by his grandparents."

"Is he in love with you?"

"At first he had a childish crush on me, of the obsessive kind, then, as he grew, it changed into a sort of cross between romantic love and physical desire. He's very dangerous, you know."

"Come on! Harry Potter?"

"Just listen. Only about a month ago, I happened to find

myself alone with him. I'd gone to Carlo's place for dinner, but when I got there he hadn't come home yet, and so I waited for him in the living room. Arturo, who doesn't live with his father, arrived a few minutes later. He sat down beside me on the sofa and started to talk to me, every so often stroking my shoulder with a trembling hand. It was hypnotic. Five minutes later—"

"He had his hands all over you."

"Wrong. And you know what? It was me who was about to put my hands all over him."

"Really?"

"Really. You have no idea how powerful the energy of desire emanating from his whole body is. It's an irresistible sex appeal. Every time his fingers grazed my shoulder I shuddered all over. I was able to control myself because I kept reminding myself I was twice his age, which is a pretty stupid reason. Anyway, he sort of frightened me. Fortunately then Carlo arrived."

"Does he have a girlfriend?"

"Who, Arturo? No, not that I know of. And I don't think that he . . . I think he's very shy with girls. And he doesn't seem to have any friends. At any rate, it seems like you also found him pretty interesting."

"Yes, very interesting. He said he lives here in Vigàta."

"That's right."

"Have you ever been to his place?"

She giggled.

"Never. If I had, it would have been a disaster."

"Do you know what part of Vigàta he lives in?"

"No."

"What does he do, other than study philosophy?"

"No idea. I can find out, if you like."

"No, no. I may be curious, but not so curious as to pry into his private life."

"End of subject?"

"End of subject."

"So I can go now?"

"Why?" asked Montalbano, bewildered.

She didn't answer, but only put her arm on his shoulder, pulled him towards her and kissed him on the lips.

"When you called me to invite me to dinner—since I know it certainly wasn't because of my, so to speak, feminine graces—I wondered what you wanted from me. And now I realize that it was because you needed some information about Arturo."

"But it was you who got me to talk about him."

"Yes, but you're a clever one, Inspector Montalbano."

"You're pretty shrewd yourself."

"Anyway, now that you've got your information, I'm no longer needed, and so I can go. Isn't that right?"

"Well, yes and no."

"Explain."

"It's true that I wanted some information about Arturo, but that wasn't the only reason I invited you. Normally when

I want to know something from someone, I summon them to the police station, I don't invite them to dinner."

"Well, by inviting me to dinner, I guess you were mixing business with pleasure, no? I supposedly being the pleasure?"

"Why are you using clichés? They lead you to false conclusions. In fact you're not the 'pleasure.'"

"Not even?"

"Let me finish. You're a beautiful woman and a friend whom I trust very dearly and like to spend time with every now and then, talking and laughing . . . It's not a relationship 'for pleasure,' and I think to call it that is to diminish it a great deal."

"The only blot in your little speech is that 'every now and then.'"

"Give me a break, Ingrid, you're not going to tell me you wish you could see me every day!"

"If the two of us ever became lovers and were always together, day and night, I think one of us would end up killing the other."

"You see? You're starting to get it. The truth is that by getting together now and then, the way we do, we're able to comfort each other."

Ingrid made a bewildered face.

"I really can't see myself as a charity worker, I'm sorry."

"And me, yes?"

"Not on your life!"

"And yet that's the way it is. We give each other mutual comfort."

"Comfort for what?"

"For loneliness, Ingrid."

Out of the blue Ingrid started crying uncontrollably. This time it was Montalbano who embraced her and held her tight. After barely five minutes, however, her bout of melancholy had passed. She was like the sparrows in the rain that shake it off and a minute later they're dry again.

"Did I ever tell you the story about that member of parliament who asked me to go to bed with him?"

"That doesn't seem to me like such an unusual proposition."

"Right, but he wanted us to get dressed up first—he as a priest and me as a nun."

They got three fourths of the way through the second bottle, and when they got up because it was past two o'clock, Ingrid could barely stand up straight. Nor did Montalbano feel much like driving her back to Montelusa, since they would probably end up crashing into a tree or another car. In the end Ingrid came to bed with him and fell asleep in the twinkling of an eye. The inspector, on the other hand, spent an hour of hell with that woman lying next to him, her scent of apricot growing stronger by the minute. He only managed to fall asleep after getting as far away from her as he could, with half his body hanging over the edge of the bed and continually in danger of falling off. And he kept waking up every fifteen minutes. Finally at a certain point he went and lay down on the sofa in the living room. But it was too uncomfortable, and so a short while later he went and returned to the torture grill. Saint Salvo, burnt alive by the fires of temptation.

11

He was awakened some time after nine by Adelina making noise in the kitchen. Ingrid, however, didn't move. He couldn't even hear her breathing.

During her sleep she had uncovered herself and had a breast exposed and an extremely long leg sticking out from under the sheet. Montalbano dutifully covered everything back up.

He felt uneasy. It would be the first time his housekeeper saw a woman in his bed, aside from the few times Livia had been there—since Adelina, who'd taken an immediate dislike to her, normally stopped coming whenever Livia came to stay for a few days.

It was true that Adelina had made the bed a few times before when Ingrid had slept there, but making the bed was one thing, and finding a naked woman in it was something else.

He got up quietly and went to Adelina in the kitchen.

"Coffee's ready, *dottori*."

Still groggy from all the whisky he'd drunk and the restless night he'd just had, he drank two cups in a row.

"Shou' I take a some a the young lady, or you take a ta ha youssel'?"

Apparently upon arriving she'd taken a peek to see if he'd already gone out and seen Ingrid in bed with him.

Montalbano looked at her. And in the housekeeper's eyes he noticed a glimmer, ever so tiny, of satisfaction. And he knew why. Adelina was pleased that he had been unfaithful to Livia, or at least so she thought.

For whatever reason, he felt obliged to explain things to her.

"You see, we had a lot to drink last night, and she was in no condition to drive. . . ." he started out.

But Adelina interrupted him with a wave of the hand.

"*Dottori*, wha' you tellin' a me fuh? You don' need a 'splain a nuttin' a me. You gotta do whatta you gotta do, *e basta*! Anyways, a pretty woman inna flesh allaways a better 'n' a dolls you hadda before."

Mortified, realizing he would never manage to explain the business of the dolls to her, Montalbano grabbed the cup of coffee and went to wake up Ingrid.

When he entered the station that morning, he had no idea that just a few hours later the dead calm would come to an end.

"Ahh Chief! 'Ere's 'at kid come onna part o' Signura Sciosciostrommi waitin' f'yiz."

Imagine Arturo ever wasting any time!

"Show him in."

Montalbano didn't even manage to sit down before the kid came in, so excited he forgot to say hello.

"I've figured it all out!" he proclaimed triumphantly.

"How'd you do it?"

"I realized that the place where they make lamb's head could only be a tavern or something similar. So I asked around and found out that there's a wine shop outside of Gallotta where they also serve food, and then I went there. But it was too late in the day to take a walk in the area. And so I went back at dawn this morning."

"At dawn? Really?"

"I couldn't sleep, I swear. Anyway, I started walking around at random and all of a sudden I came to a tiny little lake with water the color of the sky, and nearby there's a ruin of a small house. I think both places correspond perfectly with the clues in the poem."

"Well done. And did you come away with any impressions, any ideas that might be of use?"

The kid's face expressed his disappointment.

"No, unfortunately."

"So all we can do is wait."

"So it seems. But I really don't understand the meaning of this stage in the game."

"Me neither."

"If anything comes up, will you let me know?"

"Of course, since you're in a position to save me time and effort."

About an hour later, Catarella rang him.

"Chief, 'at'd be a Signuri Billiardo want'n' a ripport 'is dissippearance insomuch azza owner of 'is car."

"He wants to report his own disappearance?"

"Nossir, not 'is own as Signuri Billiardo 'isself, Chief."

"Then whose?"

"As pertainin' to 'is car 'at belongs ta him, Chief."

"I see. A case of auto theft, then."

"Azackly, Chief."

"And you're busting my balls over a stolen car? Put the call through to Fazio."

"The probblem's 'at Bigliardo assists on talkin' t'yiz poissonally in poisson."

"All right, put him on."

"I can't put 'im on, Chief, insomuch as—"

"—he's on the premises? Then show him in."

"Good morning," the man said, coming forward with his hand extended.

Well dressed, about fifty, handkerchief in breast pocket, gold-rimmed glasses, salt-and-pepper hair cut extremely short, English shoes all curlicues, mustache with the ends waxed and curled up. He was so drenched in cologne that the room immediately filled up with a sweet scent that turned the stomach. The mere sight of him aroused such antipathy in the inspector that he just let the man's hand hang in the air, without shaking it. He decided to deal with the matter in his own way.

"*Comment allez-vous?*" he asked the man.

The other looked at him as if he'd been kidnapped by Barbary pirates.

"Ah, you mean you're not French? Really? Hmph . . . !" said Montalbano, sizing him up very slowly.

"Excuse me for just one second," he said a moment later.

He got up and went over to the window and opened it. He looked around a little outside, then came and sat back down behind his desk.

"I'm sorry to trouble you, but I wanted to—" the man began, a little uncertain.

"Ah, if you'd be so kind, give me just one more second."

He bent down, opened the bottom drawer of his desk, pulled out a memo at random, studied it for a long time, grabbed a pen, corrected two words, then put it back, and closed the drawer again. After which he looked at Billiardo with a far-off look in his eyes.

"You were saying . . ."

"I want to report—"

"Were you hurt?"

The man balked.

"Was I hurt? . . . No."

"I'm sorry, I'd understood that you'd been hit by a car, Signor Billiardo."

"Vilardo."

He'd had his fun.

"So tell me."

"I'm here to report the theft of my car," he said, curling with two fingers the left-hand tip of his mustache.

"What kind of car is it?"

"An SUV, a—"

"You drive an SUV here in town?"

"Yes, sometimes, but I have two cars."

"When was it stolen?"

"The day before yesterday."

"Why didn't you report it immediately?"

"Because I thought my son Pietro had taken it without telling me, which he often does."

Montalbano couldn't resist the urge to perform a little.

"I'm sorry, let me get this straight. You have two cars and your son Pietro doesn't have any?"

"Well, yes."

"Does he live with you?"

"Yes."

"How old is he?"

"Thirty."

"A big baby, in other words."

The man opened his eyes wide.

"I don't understand."

"Don't you remember how one of our ministers defined these thirty-year-olds who still live at home? He called them 'big babies.'"

Vilardo looked at him with increasing befuddlement. He was starting to have serious doubts about the inspector's mental health.

"I don't see what that has to do with—"

"You're absolutely right, go on."

"Where were we?"

"You were saying the big baby often takes your SUV."

"Ah, yes. The only problem was that Pietro told me he'd gone to Palermo in a friend's car."

"All right. That seems good enough to me. Now I'll send you to someone who will register your report."

"Just a minute, Inspector. It was you I wanted to talk to, and for a specific reason. I wanted to tell you that yesterday I saw my car again, here in Vigàta, but only from a distance."

"Are you sure it was yours?"

"Absolutely certain."

"Could you see who was driving?"

"A man, but I couldn't make out his features. On top of everything else, it was getting dark. But he wasn't alone, because at a certain point I saw a head of blond hair appear from the back, as if a woman had been lying down on the backseat and suddenly sat up. But the man driving shoved her back down violently. Then a bus passed that—"

"Probably a couple quarreling."

He picked up the receiver.

"Catarella? Come to my office and take Signor Vilardo to Fazio's office."

Less than an hour later, Catarella informed him, in a low voice, that there was a man at the desk whose name he hadn't understood because the man was crying, saying he wanted to talk to the inspector.

The moment he entered, Montalbano instantly realized that the man—a wretched, poorly dressed fifty-year-old—could barely stand up. His eyes were red and swollen from weeping, and he kept wiping them with a dirty handker-chief. The inspector shot to his feet, put an arm around the man's shoulders, and sat him down in one of the chairs in front of the desk.

"Would you like some water?"

The man nodded yes. Montalbano filled a glass from a bottle on top of the filing cabinet and handed it to him. The man drank it all in one draught.

"I'm sorry, I've been running around . . . since early this morning, when it was still dark outside, and I'm so tired I could die."

Two big tears welled up in his eyes, and the man wiped them away, looking slightly embarrassed.

"My daughter . . . my . . ."

His voice cracked and he was unable to speak.

"What's your name, sir?"

"Giuseppe Bonmarito."

"Listen, Signor Bonmarito, no need to force yourself,

we've got all the time in the world. Just try to calm down. You can start talking when you feel up to it."

"Could . . . could I?" the man asked, holding up the empty glass.

Montalbano got up, went back and filled it. Bonmarito drank half of it, took a deep breath, and began talking.

"Since yesterday afternoon, my daughter Ninetta . . ."

"Hasn't been heard from?"

"Yes . . ."

For the moment, and for as long as he remained in a state of confusion, it was best just to ask him only questions requiring short answers.

"Has this happened before?"

"Never."

"How old is she?"

"Just turned eighteen."

"Does she have a job?"

"No, she's a student. Last year of high school."

"Does she have any brothers or sisters?"

"She's our only child."

"Does she have a boyfriend?"

"A real boyfriend, no. There's a boy who's always running after her. But I think my daughter considers him just a friend."

"Do you know him?"

"Yes. And last night I went to see him, woke him up, in fact, but he said he hadn't seen Ninetta since the morning. They're schoolmates."

"What time did she go out?"

"My wife said it was a little before six. She was supposed to go to the movies with a girlfriend and should have been back home no later than eight-thirty."

"Have you spoken with this friend of hers?"

The poor man seemed a little revived now.

"Yes, I have. We waited for Ninetta till nine-thirty, before sitting down to eat, and when she didn't turn up, I called her girlfriend and she told me that she and Ninetta had split up right after the movie, which was around eight o'clock."

"Which movie theater was it?"

"The Splendor."

"Have you got a photograph of your daughter?"

"Yessir."

The man took a small picture out of his wallet and handed it to him. Blond, smiling, beautiful.

"There's a slight problem," said Montalbano.

"What's that?" Bonmarito asked, alarmed.

"Your daughter's legally an adult."

"So what?"

"I mean we can't take any action before a certain amount of time has passed."

"Why not?"

"Because it's possible she went away of her own volition. Know what I mean? And, theoretically, being a legal adult, she needn't account to anyone for what she does."

The man lowered his head and stared at his shoe tops. Then he looked up at Montalbano.

"No," he said decisively.

"No what?"

"She's much too attached to her mother. And my wife is very sick with heart problems. Even if she ran away with a man, she would at least have given us a call."

Bonmarito said these words with such conviction and certainty that Montalbano was persuaded. Which aggravated the situation, because it meant that if Ninetta hadn't phoned, it was because she was in no condition to do so.

"Does your daughter have a cell phone?"

"Yessir."

"Have you tried calling her?"

"Of course. But it's turned off."

"Where did you go looking for her?"

"I took the first bus, the five A.M., and made the rounds of all the hospitals and clinics, went to the police commissioner's office and the carabinieri in Montelusa, then I even went to the carabinieri's station in Vigàta, I came here, and I went around asking people on the street if anyone had seen her last night. . . ."

He couldn't go on. This time he started sobbing silently, holding his handkerchief one minute over his mouth, the next minute over his eyes.

Montalbano picked up the picture of the girl again. She was so beautiful! That blond hair . . .

Then all at once, in a flash, Vilardo's words came back to him: *I saw a head of blond hair appear from the back. . . .*

He shot to his feet, so suddenly that Bonmarito automatically stood up with him.

"No, no, please stay. I'll be right back."

He pushed Fazio's door open with such force that he felt like Catarella making one of his triumphal entrances.

"That guy . . . what's his name . . . Vilardo, did he leave a telephone number?"

"Yes, his home phone and his cell phone."

"Call him immediately. Ask him to tell you exactly where he was last night when he saw his stolen car drive by, and what direction it went in. Then come straight to my office."

He went back to his room. Bonmarito was resting his elbows on his knees and had his face in his hands.

"Listen, give me your address and telephone number. I also want the addresses and telephone numbers of that boy she knows from school and her girlfriend, the one she went to the movies with."

Bonmarito dictated them to him.

"If you were to receive any ransom demands . . ."

The man made a smile so tense, the inspector felt his heart give a tug.

"Ransom?" the man said. "We're dirt poor."

"Where do you work?"

"At the fish market. I'm a guard."

"Anyway, anything new comes up, call me at once, don't waste any time. Now go home to your wife, don't leave her alone."

Bonmarito got out of his chair ever so slowly, as if every movement was an effort. He must have been at the end of his rope.

"I promise you," said Montalbano, putting a hand on the man's shoulder, "that we'll start looking for her right away, even if it's not official. Do you have a car?"

Another smile more eloquent than any reply.

He brought the man to Catarella.

"Ring Gallo and tell him to give Signor Bonmarito a ride home."

"I spoke with the engineer."

"What engineer?"

"Vilardo. He told me that yesterday evening, at what must have been around eight-twenty, no later, his SUV drove past the little park in Via del Sambuco, where he was walking his dog."

"Did he see what direction the car was going in?"

"He thought it turned right, in the direction of Via dei Glicini. But he's not sure, because at that moment a bus drove past and blocked his view. Would you please explain to me what's going on?"

The inspector told him what Bonmarito had come to see him about and showed him the photo of the girl. Fazio looked at it a long time and then handed it back to the inspector, twisting up his face.

"If they're poor and she's so beautiful, there can only be one reason why she was kidnapped."

"I agree. What do you suggest?"

"You don't want to wait the allotted time established by the law?"

"No."

"You're right. But in my opinion, we must first determine whether the girl was consenting."

"You're imagining an elopement?"

"That's not what they call it anymore, but it's the same idea."

"The father rules that out. He's absolutely certain that, because of the mother's illness, even if she did run away, she would have got in touch by now."

"Let's forget about the mother and father."

"Why?"

"Chief, just the other night on TV they showed some kid who'd cut the throats of an old couple just to rob them of twenty euros. And you know what the killer's mother said? She said her son was an angel who would never even kill a worm."

"But Vilardo did notice that, when the woman in the backseat tried to sit up, the guy pushed her back down."

"So what? Maybe she was being careless by sitting up and the guy made her lie back down, telling her to be more careful or somebody might see her."

"But if they wanted to leave town together and cover

their tracks, wasn't it a mistake to steal a car? When a girl who's a legal adult runs away, we're not obliged to intervene, but when a car is stolen, we are."

"That's certainly true. But it's possible that it was absolutely necessary for them to steal the car, despite the risk."

"Why are you so insistent on the possibility that she ran away with someone?"

"Because kidnappings are really rare around here. Not to mention that she's the daughter of a man who hasn't got anything but his eyes to cry with . . ."

"But you don't rule out the possibility that it could be a kidnapping for the purpose of rape."

"Right. That, unfortunately, is the second possibility we have to keep in mind."

12

"And therefore you don't rule out the biggest danger," Montalbano continued, "which is that whoever kidnapped her will keep her for a few days at his complete disposal and then kill her and drop the body off somewhere for us to find her."

"Why kill her? He could just as easily set her free!"

"No! The girl will have seen what he looks like! Vilardo didn't say the guy was driving with a ski mask on! And so, by setting her free, the kidnapper would run the risk that she would report him and be able to identify him. No, believe me, he would kill her."

"That's also true."

"Listen, let's at least do something to set our minds at rest. Do you know where the Cinema Splendor is?"

"Yes."

"Ninetta came out a little after eight o'clock. Ask some people who live in the neighborhood and a few local shop owners if they saw or heard anything unusual last night. And bring the girl's picture with you."

"And what are you going to do?"

"I'm going to eat and then pay a visit to"—he looked at the sheet of paper in front of him—"Lina Anselmo, who's apparently the friend Ninetta went to the movies with last night."

He ate hardly anything. The thought of Bonmarito, that poor father so dignified in his despair, wouldn't let him get much past his lips.

After finishing his lunch, he got in the car and drove off. He always preferred giving no advance warning before his visits. That way nobody had the time to prepare any answers to his questions. He'd learned from experience that everyone he interrogated, every last person, even the most innocent and honest, would always try to appear a little different from the way they were, a little straighter, a little more proper.

Lina Anselmo, the girl who'd gone to the movies with Ninetta, lived almost outside of town, on the top floor of a block of flats without an elevator. Montalbano went up the stairs without cursing, since the climb took the place of his customary walk along the jetty.

A rather homely girl of about eighteen, very skinny, with her hair in a bun, and wearing glasses, opened the door as far as the chain would allow.

"Are you Lina Anselmo?"

"And who are you?"

"Inspector Montalbano, police."

"What do you want?"

"To talk about Ninetta."

"All right."

"But you have to let me in."

"No."

"Why not?"

"Because Papa doesn't want me to let strangers inside."

"Is your father there?"

"No."

"Is your mother?"

"Neither. I'm alone."

Cursing to himself, Montalbano pulled his identification card out of his pocket and handed it to her. Lina took it with two fingers.

"Study it carefully. You'll see I really am with the police."

She barely glanced at it and gave it back to him.

"That doesn't mean anything."

"What do you mean?!"

"It could be fake."

What to do? Break open the door with his shoulder? And what if she started screaming like a pig at the slaughter? Should he send for some of his uniformed men?

There was probably no point. The little idiot might think the uniforms were fake, too. The best thing was to get it over with as quickly as possible.

"Yesterday evening, did you go to the movies with Ninetta Bonmarito?"

"Yes."

"Do you often go to the movies together?"

"Yes."

"Does anyone ever bother you during the movie?"

"Yes."

"What do you do when that happens?"

"We change seats."

"And what if there aren't any empty seats?"

"Ninetta prefers that we leave."

"Did anyone approach you two last night?"

"No, nobody."

"What time was it when you came out of the theater?"

"A little after eight."

"Did anyone follow you?"

"No."

"And you, Lina, how did you get home?"

"I have a scooter."

"And why didn't you give Ninetta a ride home?"

"I usually do."

"And why didn't you yesterday?"

"Because I had to get home a little earlier than usual to help Mamma. We were having friends over to dinner."

"Listen, are you the only person Ninetta goes to the movies with?"

"No, sometimes she goes with Lucia, another friend."

"Finally, do you have any idea what might have happened to her?"

"No, none. And I've thought about it a lot."

"Listen, does Ninetta confide in you?"

"Of course."

"Did she ever tell you she was in love with anyone, or whether anyone had propositioned her, or—"

"There weren't any boys or men in Ninetta's life. The only one she sort of liked was Michele, Michele Guarnera. And that's all. Do you want to come in?" she asked unexpectedly, removing the chain and opening the door wide.

She'd been convinced.

"No," said Montalbano.

He turned his back and started descending the stairs. The girl was ugly, stubborn, and distrustful, but definitely sincere.

The Guarnera family lived on the third floor of a modern building in a brand-new neighborhood of Vigàta. The cars one saw parked on the street were mostly expensive models for people with money. There were even well-tended little gardens. He buzzed the intercom. A polite-sounding woman with a nice voice answered.

"Inspector Montalbano here, police."

Sparkling clean lobby, with an elevator to boot. A good-looking woman of about forty answered the door. She was well dressed and smiled only with the corners of her mouth, as her eyes looked worried.

"Please come in."

A tasteful living room. Modern furniture. The inspector noticed a print by Cagli and a painting by Guttuso.

"Is there any news of Ninetta?" the woman asked straight off.

"No, not yet. Are you Michele's mother?"

"Yes, my name is Anna."

"Pleased to meet you, signora. Is your son at home?"

"Yes, but he's still asleep."

Still asleep at that hour of the afternoon? The kid certainly took things easy! But Anna was quick to explain.

"Ninetta's father came here late last night, just before one A.M., when we were already asleep. It gave us a terrible fright, since my husband is away in Rome for work. Anyway, after that Michele was unable to fall back asleep, and he finally collapsed about two hours ago. Should I wake him up?"

"Unfortunately, yes."

"Would you like a coffee?"

"No need to bother, thank you."

Michele took about five minutes to come out. He was wearing jeans, a half-open shirt, and slippers. His hair was a mess and his face still wet from the quick washing he'd given it. A big strapping lad with the shoulders of a rugby player and an intelligent look about him.

"I'll leave you two alone to talk," said the mother.

Montalbano appreciated her discretion.

"You begin," he said to the youth when they were alone.

Michele seemed a little disconcerted by the suggestion. He looked at the inspector and said nothing.

"Well?"

"But aren't you supposed to ask me the questions?"

"Normally, yes, when I'm at the station. But this time I'd rather you spoke first, and freely."

"Where should I begin?"

"Wherever you like."

The youth couldn't make up his mind. Montalbano gave him a little nudge.

"Talk to me about Ninetta."

"Ninetta . . . a wonderful girl. So close to her family, especially her mother. She's very worried about her. She's like someone from another time."

"In what sense?"

"Well, she's the first in her class, and yet in spite of that, everybody likes her because she's not a nerd and she's always willing to help her classmates. She's very beautiful but she's not conceited, she's not a showoff."

"And outside of school, do you and she get together with other classmates?"

"Sure, we often have parties."

"And how does Ninetta act on those occasions?"

"She's very cheerful and sociable, always joking around, but she also knows how to keep away people who push too far."

"So, at these parties . . ."

"I see what you're getting at. She doesn't drink, doesn't smoke, doesn't do joints, and doesn't make a show of herself. What more could you want?"

"Are you in love with her?"

"Yes."

He'd said it without the slightest hesitation. With a certain pride, in fact.

"What about her?"

"Her, no. She likes me well enough, likes my company and all that, but no, she's not in love with me."

"Do you know whether she's had any affairs in the past?"

The youth gave a little laugh.

"Inspector, maybe I haven't made myself clear enough. I'll try to be as direct as possible. Ninetta's girlfriends are always teasing her because she's the only virgin left in the class."

"As far as you know, was there anyone chasing after her?"

"Everybody."

"Anyone a little more aggressively than the others?"

"Francesco. A few months ago Ninetta slapped him."

"Why?"

"It happened at a party. Since he'd had a bit to drink, he said to Ninetta, right in front of everyone, what he'd like to do with her if he could spend the night with her."

"And how did it end up?"

"Well, she started slapping him and we intervened and tried to get them to make up, but since then they aren't speaking to each other."

"Is he a friend of yours?"

"He's in the second track."

"Do you know where he lives?"

"Yes. His last name's Diluigi. But believe me, he's not the kind of person who—"

"I'll be the judge of that. Let me have the address."

Michele told him.

"And where were you yesterday evening? Sorry, but I have to ask you."

"I understand. You want to know my alibi. I spent the afternoon in Montelusa. I play tennis. At least seven or eight people must have seen me."

"And after that?"

"When I got back to Vigàta it must have been around seven-thirty."

"Ninetta was kidnapped shortly after eight."

"Wait. On my way back, my scooter wasn't running right, and so I took it straight to the shop. They told me to come back in an hour to pick it up, and so I went home, dropped off my gym bag, changed because I was in a sweat-suit, and then went back out to pick up my scooter. If you want I can give you the mechanic's address."

"No, there's no need, thanks. Have anything else to tell me?"

The youth thought about this for a minute.

"Well, I'm not sure it's important . . ."

"Tell me anyway."

"About a month ago, Ninetta told me she'd been assaulted."

"Can you be more precise?"

"She was on her way home and was a little late because she'd been studying at a friend's house and it was raining and already dark. The street was deserted, and at a certain point some guy came up beside her, pushed her inside a doorway, put his hand over her mouth, turned her around towards the wall, and started pulling up her skirt. Ninetta was so terrified she didn't even have the strength to react. Luckily a man was coming down the stairs just then, and so the guy ran away. Ninetta also told me that, despite getting so scared, she didn't want her parents to know."

"Why not?"

"Because she was afraid they wouldn't let her go out alone anymore. They're very protective of her."

"Did she describe her attacker to you?"

"No."

"Where did this happen?"

"She didn't say. Do you think it might have been the same guy, trying again?"

Montalbano threw up his hands. After a pause, the youth looked the inspector in the eye, then lowered his gaze, then looked at him again.

"Do you think there's any hope we'll find her alive?"

He was obviously of the same mind as Montalbano. Whoever it was, after using and abusing her, would surely kill her.

"I certainly want there to be."

"I'm going to pay them a visit today," said Michele.

"Pay whom a visit?"

"Ninetta's parents. I don't like leaving them all alone."

While he was at it, he decided to go and pay a call on the kid who'd been cuffed by Ninetta. Luckily the Diluigis didn't live very far from the Guarneras, in a fancy building in a fancy neighborhood. Fifth floor. He took the elevator, rang the doorbell, and a hulk of about six-foot-three in a tank top came and opened the door. He was angry and talked as if he was about to bite.

"If you're selling something, we never buy a fucking thing, and we pay all our bills at the bank."

He was about to shut the door when Montalbano stuck a foot inside and blocked it.

"Remove that foot or I'll break it."

"Calm down. I'm not selling anything and I don't have any bills for you to pay. I'm Inspector Montalbano, police."

"Yeah, and?"

"I want to talk to Francesco Diluigi. Is he your son?"

"Unfortunately, yes."

"Well?"

"Come in."

The entrance hall was tidy and welcoming.

"Carmelina! Come quick!" the man yelled.

A woman of slightly greater heft than the man appeared. Red-haired, bespectacled, and unkempt, she was wearing a sweatsuit that sagged in every direction.

"This gentleman is a police inspector and wants to talk to you about your precious little boy," the man said, leaving the entranceway.

"What can I do for you?" the woman said. "So you are . . . ?"

"Inspector Montalbano."

"Inspector of what?"

"I'm with the police."

"My son is an angel," the woman was keen to point out before anything else, assuming an air of defiance and putting her hands on her ample hips.

"I don't doubt it for a minute, signora."

But the woman insisted.

"My son couldn't possibly have done anything wrong."

"Of that I'm convinced, signora."

"My son . . ."

". . . is a rare pearl."

"That's exactly right!"

"Can I see him?"

"No."

"He's not at home?"

"He is. But he's been in bed with a fever since this morning. He would like to get up, but I won't let him."

"Why not?"

"The change in temperature might make him sicker."

"All right then, I'll go to his room myself."

"I don't think that's a good idea. You don't know what Francesco's like! He might get scared."

"Of what?"

"He's very sensitive! And defenseless. He might get frightened to see a police inspector appear at his bedside. Do you really have to tell him?"

"Tell him what?"

"That you're an inspector. Can't you pretend you're the doctor I called, who hasn't arrived yet?"

"Out of the question."

She looked at Montalbano with the expression of a person about to lay her head on the executioner's chopping block. He realized it was hopeless, and heaved a sigh of resignation.

"All right, then. Come with me."

But when they entered the room, the boy wasn't in his bed.

"He must have gone to the bathroom. He has a little diarrhea. I'll go give him a hand."

Give him a hand at what? Wiping his heinie?

"In the meantime you can make yourself comfortable."

In the room it was beastly hot. There was a small electric heater in the corner, turned on. Aside from the bed, there was a small wardrobe, a bookcase, a small worktable with a computer on it, turned off, and a chair.

Montalbano started looking at the books.

The ones on the top shelf interested him the most: *Venus in Furs*, *Justine*, *The Story of O*, a treatise on sexual psychopathology, two leather-bound years' worth of *Penthouse* . . . He must work a lot with his hands, the rare pearl. The mother returned.

"He'll be here in just a minute. I see you're looking at his books. Just imagine, neither I nor my husband have ever even opened a book, except for the ones they gave us at school. But him! D'you see how many he has? He just loves books. I tell him he's going to ruin his eyes one day, but he won't hear of it. And he doesn't want anyone ever to touch them. He dusts them off himself. All he ever does is read and sit at the computer."

Looking at porno sites, no doubt.

"And his teachers don't understand him! They're jealous of his intelligence and purposely give him bad grades!"

At last Francesco arrived, in pajamas and slippers and a woolen blanket wrapped around him. As he was getting back into bed with the loving help of his mother, the first question that popped into the inspector's head was:

"How do you manage to stand up?"

Because Francesco, big and bulky as he was, didn't look like he was made of flesh and blood, but of some sort of yellowy chicken gelatin, to be exact, which quivered all over with every move he made and seemed to lose its texture.

"Don't tire him out," his mother advised, lying down in bed alongside her little jewel.

Was she planning on staying there for the questioning?

"I'm sorry, signora, but I would like to speak with your son alone," Montalbano said, polite but firm.

"But I am his mother!"

"I have never had the slightest doubt of that, signora, but I'm asking you please to leave just the same."

"No!"

"Oh, all right." The inspector sighed.

Then, turning to Francesco:

"That day at the party, when Ninetta slapped you—"

"What are you saying?" said the woman, springing to her feet.

Then she turned to Francesco, who seemed to be melting before their eyes, and asked:

"Who dared?"

"Mamma, come on, leave us alone," said Francesco.

Without saying a word, and with eyes shooting flames, the mother indignantly headed for the door. But before going out, she turned and said:

"And this is the thanks I get, Francesco, for everything I do for you every minute of the day?"

And she slammed the door behind her. At the theater it would have been a great exit line worthy of applause, no doubt.

13

"Did . . . did Ninetta report me?" Francesco asked in a now liquefied voice.

"Nobody reported you."

But why was he still wasting time with this worm?

"Just answer one question for me and then I'll go. Do you know how to drive?"

"I don't have my license."

"I didn't ask you whether you had your license, I asked if you know how to drive."

"No, I don't. I don't even know how to drive a motorbike."

Montalbano opened the door to leave and very nearly smashed it into the face of the signora, who was crouching down, listening and spying through the keyhole. She raced into her son's room, and Montalbano let himself out of the apartment.

He was furious at himself. Michele had tried to tell him what kind of person Francesco was, but he wouldn't listen. If he had, it would have saved him some time.

"Anyone call for me?"

"F'yiz poissonally in poisson, no."

"Then send me Fazio."

"'E in't onna premisses, Chief."

"Then send me Inspector Augello."

"'E in't onna premisses neither."

"So where is he?"

"Witta foresaid Fazio, Chief."

The moment he sat down, the inspector picked up the receiver to call Bonmarito, just to stay in touch and let him know that he was working hard to find his daughter. But he immediately put the phone back down.

He suddenly didn't have the courage. If the guy started asking questions, what was he going to tell him? That things were looking pretty bleak?

Yes, because from everything he'd been told first by Lina and then by Michele, this was the very conclusion he had drawn, unfortunately. That the girl had been kidnapped not by a jilted boyfriend or a rejected suitor, but by someone Ninetta may well have never seen before. Ninetta had had the bad luck to walk into the path of someone out looking for a girl to kidnap, any girl at all. Well, maybe not just any girl; maybe she had to have certain qualities, and if it hadn't been Ninetta, someone who looked like her would have been just fine. If it was someone from Ninetta's circle of friends, he would certainly have known that there was no point lying in wait around the movie house, because Lina would inevitably give Ninetta a ride home on her scooter. Except that night she didn't. But the kidnapper couldn't have known this. Unless we were to assume complicity between Lina and the kidnapper, but that seemed impossible. In conclusion, there wasn't a single starting point that might in some way limit the scope of the investigation.

Mimì and Fazio came in at the same time.

"Where were you guys?"

"You tell him," Mimì said brusquely to Fazio. "I've got something I need to take care of. See you later this evening."

And he dashed out of the office without saying goodbye. He seemed worried and upset. Montalbano looked on with a touch of astonishment as he closed the door behind him.

"What's wrong with him?" he asked Fazio.

"I dunno. He got all touchy when I started talking to him about the missing girl."

"And why'd you talk to him about her?"

"Why, wasn't I supposed to?"

"That's not what I'm saying, I just want to know how you happened to talk to him about the kidnapping. You know, like, what brought it up?"

The question had a precise reason behind it. Despite the fact that they'd been working together for so many years, you couldn't really say that Augello and Fazio communicated much between them.

"I had to, Chief. I'll explain. When I got back from making those rounds you asked me to do—"

"Speaking of which, did you find anything out?"

"Nobody noticed anything, though two of the shop-keepers were already closing up."

"Big surprise there!"

"But do you know where the Splendor is located?"

"Not exactly, no."

"It's a brand-new cinema in the New Vigàta, on a street with five shops and four apartment buildings, one of which is ready and the other three not rented out yet."

"How did Ninetta get there, I wonder? She hasn't even got a scooter."

"I'm sure she took the circle line, which stops on a street parallel to the one the cinema's on."

"Therefore when they said goodbye outside the theater, her friend drove off on her scooter, while Ninetta must have headed for the street where the bus stops."

"Right."

"We have to do something, Fazio, and fast. As soon as we're done talking, I want you to go to the urban transporta-tion management offices and get the name of whoever was working the circle line around eight last night. Track him down, show him the girl's picture, and ask him if he saw her getting on the bus at that stop."

"There's one problem. I don't have the photo anymore. Inspector Augello asked for it and I gave it to him."

"Why'd he want it?"

"He didn't say."

Montalbano remained pensive for a moment. Then he made up his mind.

"Go to bus management anyway, without the photograph. Describe her to the driver. A pretty girl like that, people are going to remember her. Now continue what you were saying about Mimì."

"So, as I was saying, when I got back, Inspector Augello came into my office for some information and he saw Nina's photograph. He picked it up, looked at it closely, and asked me why I had it, so I told him the whole story. He wanted to know everything. Then the phone rang. It was someone calling to say there was a car on fire near the sixth kilometer of the provincial road to Montereale. They even said it looked like an SUV."

An SUV? Montalbano pricked up his ears.

"And then Augello said he was coming with me," Fazio concluded.

"So what was it?"

"When we got there the car was still burning. It'd been abandoned in the open country, but very close to the road. We were unable to put out the fire with extinguishers. My immediate impression was that it was Vilardo's SUV. And when I was able to clean off part of the license plate, I saw that it really was Vilardo's car."

"Did you look in the trunk?"

"Yeah, but there was nothing. Luckily."

"So you too were thinking you might find Ninetta's body in there?"

"Yeah, but I called Forensics anyway."

"Why?"

"Chief, I know that the less we get Dr. Arquà mixed up in things, the better, but I thought it all out."

"You thought what out?"

"I asked myself a question. If the guy who kidnapped the girl took the SUV out to the open country to set it on fire, how did he get back? There are only two possible answers: either he has an accomplice who followed him in another car and drove him back, or he took public transportation."

"Well, he certainly didn't hitchhike."

"No, but on the other hand, there's a stop for the Vigàta bus just a few yards away."

"Come on, Fazio! So according to you the guy's gonna raise a hand and the bus is gonna pull up like nobody's business when everybody can see there's an SUV burning up just ten feet away?"

"No, Chief, that's not what I'm saying. At that moment the SUV is not burning up, it's a perfectly normal SUV that someone has driven out to the country."

"So how's the guy gonna set it on fire?"

"With a timer, Chief. The SUV catches fire, let's say, fifteen minutes after the bus has passed. That's why I called

Forensics. And it took them about a minute to confirm my theory."

"Well done, Fazio!" the inspector said with all his heart.

"Thanks, Chief."

"But all this complicates matters considerably, because it shows that the kidnapper's someone who not only has a timing device available to him, but knows how to use it. It's not like everybody in Vigàta's got timers lying about the house."

"Chief, if you know how to do it, you can turn a common alarm clock into a timing device. I know you see it all the time in American movies, but that doesn't mean it's not true."

Indeed it was true.

"But there's still another question we have to ask," said the inspector. "What need was there to torch the car? Couldn't he just have left it somewhere without setting it on fire?"

Fazio threw up his hands.

"Let's think about this for a minute. And before asking that question, there's another we should ask ourselves."

"What?"

"Why would someone need a particular kind of car, like an SUV, to kidnap somebody?"

"Well," said Fazio, "I can answer that. Apparently the place where he decided to hide the girl is somewhere in the country that can't be reached with a regular car."

"I agree with you there. But then, when he no longer needs it, why torch it? We know the car was used to transport the girl, right? But we don't know who was driving. Which means that there was something inside that car, after they used it, that would make it possible to identify him. And that was why he had to burn it up."

"There wasn't anything inside the car."

"There wasn't anything you could see with the naked eye."

"You talking about fingerprints?"

"Not only. DNA, too. You know how many traces he must have left? A shitload! This kidnapper is someone who thinks of everything. He's got a very precise, well-ordered mind. And he's making us sweat."

"Could I say something, Chief? This whole kidnapping scares me a little."

"Me too. Did you tell Vilardo he can forget about his SUV?"

"Not yet."

"Do it now. Then go immediately to the bus offices."

━━━

"Chief, 'iss 'at kid 'ass a frenn o' Signura Sciosciostrommi's onna line."

Arturo! He'd almost forgotten all about him. But he had no desire to start talking about the treasure hunt right now. There were more serious matters to think about.

"Listen, Cat, tell him I'm busy, and also tell him there's no news about that business we were talking about."

"Who, Chief?"

"Who what, Cat?"

"Whoozit 'at knows about wha' we's talkin' about? Me, him, or youse poissonally in poisson? Cuz I dunno nuttin' 'bout no bitness we's talkin' about."

The inspector felt his head spinning.

"Listen, don't tell him anything, just put the call through to me."

"I'm so sorry to disturb you, Inspector, but I'm anxious to know if there's any—"

"There's no news, unfortunately. Our friend hasn't deigned to send us any."

"Don't you find that odd?"

"I don't know what to say. But you'll have to excuse me now, I'm a little busy. Just sit tight, and I'll get back to you."

Since, as Ingrid said, the kid had no love interests or friends, he therefore had all the time in the world to waste on chickenshit.

He was about to leave to go home when Mimì Augello appeared.

"Can we talk in private for a minute?" Mimì asked.

"Certainly. Have a seat."

"Can I lock the door?"

"You can do whatever you like."

He locked the door and sat down. He seemed to be in a strange mood, between embarrassed and determined.

Montalbano helped him out.

"What's wrong, Mimì?"

"I have something confidential to tell you. I could just as easily not tell you, now that I've cleared things up, but since I think it might be useful to you, I'll tell you. Even though it costs me a great deal."

"Useful to me for what, Mimì?"

"For the investigation into the missing girl."

But he still couldn't make up his mind to tell him whatever it was that would be useful in the investigation. Montalbano realized that it was best not to force him. Then Mimì summoned his courage and spoke.

"About two months ago I went to a house of assignation."

"I don't think we've ever done a . . . ." The inspector's eyes met Mimì's and suddenly he understood.

"You mean as a client?!" he asked.

"Yes."

Then Mimì started talking very fast.

"It's a little, secluded house between here and Montelusa and it takes barely fifteen minutes to get there, and so . . . ."

Augello trailed off, as Montalbano was glaring at him.

"Asshole," said the inspector.

"I expected you would react that way. And that's why I was reluctant to tell you. But don't get the wrong idea . . . You see, I'm in love with Beba, I really am, but sometimes I just get this craving for—"

"It's not because of Beba."

"Well, why, then?"

"If you can't figure it out for yourself, then you're an even bigger asshole than I thought. What if the Montelusa police had decided to burst in that day and found you in there? Your career would have been toast."

"It didn't occur to me. Can we just forget for a second that I'm an asshole? Can I continue?"

"Go ahead."

"Among the photos that the madam was showing me of the girls available, there was one of an eighteen-year-old girl who looked exactly like Ninetta."

Montalbano felt a cold shudder. He would never have expected it. That had never figured among his hypotheses. Pretty little goody-two-shoes, all school and home, whereas . . .

But he said nothing.

"So I chose her, but the madam told me she wasn't available at that moment."

"And why did you make off with the photograph today?"

"I'll get to that. Then, about a month ago, Montelusa police raided the—"

"Wha'd I say?"

"Fine, but we also agreed to drop that line of argument."

"Sorry."

"They arrested the madam, identified all the girls and clients, and seized the photo album. The whole operation was under the command of our friend Zurlo. So I went to see Zurlo, fudged some sort of excuse, and compared Ninetta's photo with the one in the album. It's not her."

"Are you sure?"

"They look almost like twins, but it's not her. I'm absolutely sure. And that's what I had to say."

Well, if that was all, Augello could have spared himself the confession. But at least he was honest.

"What makes you think it would be useful to the investigation?"

"Well, I asked myself, what if the kidnapper mistook Ninetta for the other girl? What if he wanted to kidnap the girl in the album and grabbed Ninetta instead?"

"But wasn't the girl in the album identified?"

"She was."

"So how were you able to establish with absolute certainty that she wasn't Ninetta?"

"Because the girl in the album has a little scar under her left ear. From up close it must be clearly visible."

He pulled the photo of Ninetta out of his pocket and set it down on the desk.

"Have a look for yourself. As you can see, there's no scar on Ninetta's face. And the photo hasn't been tampered with. But from a distance you can't see the scar, which is why it could very well be a case of mistaken identity."

Great. That was all they needed, another complication. A case of mistaken identity.

"Listen, Mimì, did you manage to get the name and address of this other girl, the one in the album?"

"Yes. She lives in Vincinzella."

An old district between Vigàta and Montelusa.

"Go and pay her a visit. Talk to her."

"What do you want to know?"

"If there's any chance anyone would want to kidnap her."

"So what am I supposed to do? Go there and say, 'Er, excuse me, signorina, do you know of anyone who might want to kidnap you?'"

"Mimì, I leave it up to you to decide. You seem to have no problem whatsoever winning a woman's trust."

"I don't know, I may have lost my touch."

"Cut the crap, Mimì. There's mostly one thing I'm interested in. I want to know if there was anyone among her clients who fell in love with her, who went to see her more often than the others, or who wanted to make her leave the life she was living . . ."

"I'll give it a try."

Just as he was opening the door to his car, he heard someone call his name. It was Fazio, who'd just got back at that moment and was getting out of his car.

"You won't believe the luck, Chief!"

"Tell me."

"After informing Vilardo, I phoned the bus company and they told me that the driver of the circle line, the same one as last night, had just finished his shift and was still there in the offices. So they put him on and I asked him to wait for me. And then I went and we talked. Now wait just a sec, and I'll tell you everything."

He stuck a hand in his pocket, pulled out a small half-sheet of paper, and prepared to read it.

"If you're about to tell me the driver's name, whose son he is, and when he was born, I will make you eat that piece of paper."

Mildly mortified, Fazio—who suffered from what Montalbano called a "records-office complex"—put the paper back in his pocket, making a face that was half embarrassment, half disappointment.

"And so?"

"The driver knows Ninetta quite well. And remembers that yesterday evening around ten after eight, she got on at the stop near the Splendor. In fact, she was the only female aboard. The other three passengers were men."

"So she wasn't kidnapped there, at least."

"No. But Gibilaro—"

"Who's that?"

"The driver. Gibilaro told me that at a certain point, as he was driving down Corso De Gasperi, an SUV overtook him and, once past the bus, suddenly stopped, forcing Gibilaro to slam on the brakes, which got the passengers shouting. Then the SUV, after letting the bus pass, started following behind it."

"Wait a second. Did Gibilaro see where Ninetta was sitting?"

"Yes. She was on the left-hand side, if you're looking at the bus from behind, and she was leaning with her head against the window and looking outside, at the road."

"So it's possible that the guy driving the SUV got a look at her face as he was passing the bus?"

"Very possible."

"What then?"

"Gibilaro saw Ninetta get off at the Via delle Rose stop to catch the number three bus, which would take her close to where she lives."

Montalbano decided that it was best to go and see with his own eyes where these streets actually were. Otherwise, knowing only their names, he wouldn't have any sense of anything.

"Let's go inside," he said.

If he could sort things out right away, he would be better able to savor what Adelina had cooked for him.

14

"Ah, Chief! Ye'r back!" Catarella said joyfully.

"Yes, Cat, I'm back."

As if there could be any doubt about the matter.

"Listen," the inspector continued, "remember when, a few days ago, I left all those papers on the floor of my office?"

"Chief, beckin' yer partin' 'n' all, but there's always peppers onna floor o' y'r'office."

"Well, these ones were big topographical sheets."

Catarella looked flummoxed.

"I dunno nuttin' 'bout no top o' the graphicals, but wha' I seen was all covered wit' squiggles like road maps."

"Yeah, those are the ones I mean. Do you know where they are?"

"I's worried 'atta cleanin' laidies was gonna tro 'em aways, 'n' so I rolled 'em all up in rolls an' put 'em inna closit o' the present Fazio."

"Well done. Go get 'em."

With Fazio's help, Montalbano created the same shambles as before.

He moved all the chairs and spread the pages out on the floor, holding them in place with little boxes, staplers, and books.

"Did you manage to get a copy of the circle line's route?"

"They gave me the routes of all the buses in town."

On their floor map they traced out the route the circle line took, from the stop near the Splendor onwards.

To get the transfer to the number 3 bus, Ninetta got off at the Via delle Rose stop. Which must surely have been where she was kidnapped, because Via del Sambuco, which was where Engineer Vilardo had seen his SUV drive by, was the very next street over.

"Now give me that photo of Ninetta on my desk. . . ."

"Did Augello give it back to you?"

"Yes."

"Did he say why he'd wanted it?"

Montalbano answered vaguely.

"Apparently she looked like one of the girls somebody'd talked to him about, but he turned out to be wrong."

Fazio looked at him as though not very convinced by his reply, but said nothing.

"Take the photo yourself," the inspector continued, "and go tomorrow morning to Via delle Rose and ask around if anyone saw anything. Even though I already know it'll be a waste of time."

He went back to studying the maps.

"I forget the name of the street where Vilardo says he saw the SUV turn," said Montalbano.

"He said he thought he saw it turn right, onto Via dei Glicini."

"Let's see where this Via dei Glicini leads."

A quick glance at the map was enough for him to see.

The street ended in a small square that he already knew from having looked for it and found it a few days before. It was the same little piazza with a roundabout with exits onto four different streets: Via dei Glicini, Via Garibaldi, Via dei Mille, and Via Cavour.

"To me it seems clear," he said to Fazio, "that the kidnapper must have noticed, by chance, when he overtook the bus in Corso De Gasperi, that Ninetta was on board, or somebody he mistook for Ninetta. Or it could have been something a little more complicated, like he sees someone he knows perfectly well is not the person he's looking for but looks so much like her that she could serve as a stand-in."

"Wait a second," said Fazio. "Are you telling me that maybe the kidnapper didn't pick her out at random, as the first to come along, but had a specific model in mind?"

"That's exactly what I'm saying. It's a possibility we can't rule out. I'll continue. So he skids to a halt and lets the bus go ahead and then follows behind it. Three stops later, the girl gets off in Via delle Rose. Here the man grabs her and forces her to get inside the SUV. The car turns down Via del Sambuco. Vilardo sees it drive by and follows it with his eyes as it heads off to the right, in the direction of Via dei Glicini. But then his view is cut off by a bus."

"The number three bus, the one Ninetta was supposed to take," Fazio concluded.

"Right."

"So," Fazio continued, "if the number three bus was right behind the SUV, this means that the kidnapper moved extremely fast, grabbing the girl and forcing her into the car in a flash, before she could put up any resistance. And all this at a bus stop where there were other people waiting. How did he do it?"

"And you know what it means?"

"No."

"It means you've got another job to do," said Montalbano.

"And what's that?"

"You have to find out from the bus company who was driving the number three that night, and then go and talk to him directly and ask him if he noticed anything as he was pulling up at the stop on Via delle Rose."

"And how are we going to identify the other people waiting at the stop?"

"I think we're better off forgetting about them. If they witnessed a violent sort of scene and still haven't come forward to report it, they're never going to."

It wasn't exactly a wonderful evening. Actually the evening itself was heartbreakingly beautiful, but the problem was the inspector's bad mood managed to pollute even the landscape.

And so he ate lackadaisically on the veranda, unable to get that poor girl out of his head.

And this was a big mistake, which made him even angrier.

Compassion and pity for a human being subjected to violence and other outrages were things you should feel afterwards, once the case has been solved. Whereas, if these feelings overwhelm you during an investigation, they fog your mind, which is supposed to remain cold and lucid and keep its focus on the tormentor and not the victim.

Speaking of tormentors and victims, should he take the initiative and call Livia or not?

It was certainly his turn, since Livia had already shown her desire to make peace by calling him last time, but then unfortunately it was Ingrid who answered the phone and the whole thing spun out of control.

He got up, went inside, and dialed her number. He was immediately ambushed.

"You did it on purpose!"

"I did what on purpose?"

"You had Ingrid answer the phone!"

"Livia, how can you possibly think I would ever—"

"You're capable of anything with your Machiavellian ways!"

Pretend it's nothing and carry on.

"Livia, please, if you really care about me, just let me talk without interruption for five minutes."

"So talk."

And so they made peace. But only towards dawn. In fact the phone company bosses probably cracked open a bottle of champagne to celebrate.

At nine-thirty the following morning, Fazio was already at the station with the results of his investigation.

"You got an early start this morning."

"Chief, you know as well as I do that the more time passes, the worse it is for the girl."

"Wha'd you find out?"

"The shops in Via delle Rose closest to the bus stop were all closed already, so there was no use wasting time. Right before closing the main door for the night, the concierge of the building at 28 Via delle Rose, which is right in front of the bus stop, noticed that there were about ten people there waiting. There was even a lady she knew, and they waved at each other in greeting."

"Does she remember seeing the blond girl there?"

"She says she doesn't, no."

"And yet with Ninetta, all you have to do is see her once to remember her."

"Well, in fact, the concierge says that doesn't mean the girl wasn't there, since she didn't look at the crowd for very long."

"Did you get the coordinates of her lady friend?"

"Yes, but I haven't talked to her, I haven't had time yet. I'll go and see her as soon as we're done talking. On the other hand, I did meet with the driver of the number three line just as he was checking in to work."

"Did he see anything?"

Fazio stuck his hand in his pocket and pulled out a half-sheet of paper.

"What've you got written on that piece of paper?" the inspector asked.

"The personal particulars of the driver."

"If you read it, I'll shoot you."

"Whatever you say." Fazio sighed, resigned.

But Montalbano had to prod him to get him to resume talking.

"And so?"

"Well, when the driver pulled up at the stop, he saw an SUV with its rear end in the space reserved for the bus and a young blonde talking with someone inside the car, but sitting in back."

"Is he sure?"

"That the guy she was talking to was sitting in back? Yes, absolutely."

"Go on."

"Then the driver started looking in the mirror at the people getting on the bus, because the bus was already packed and there were a lot of people getting on, and when he closed the door in back and got ready to maneuver his way around the SUV, it suddenly pulled out ahead of him."

"And he never saw the girl after that?"

"No. And he couldn't tell me whether she got on the bus or not."

Montalbano sat there in silence.

"What are you thinking about?" Fazio asked him after a brief spell.

"I was trying to calculate the time frame."

"What do you mean?"

"I mean . . . Just listen carefully for a second. Based on what the driver told you . . . What's his name?"

"I don't remember," said Fazio, stone-faced.

"All right, all right, you can look at your goddamn piece of paper, but only to tell me his name."

Which Fazio did, grinning with satisfaction.

"Caruana, first name Antonio."

"Based on what Caruana told you, it might appear that there were two people in the SUV, one at the wheel and the other in the backseat, who would have been the one Ninetta was talking to."

"Whereas that wasn't the case?"

"I don't think so. This, in my opinion, was the work of a lone kidnapper. Who seized the girl and wants to enjoy her all by himself. He doesn't intend to share her with anyone."

"So how could he have done it?"

"That's why I said I was thinking about the time frame. So, Ninetta gets off at the three line's stop and, immediately afterwards, an SUV pulls over almost entirely in the space reserved for the bus, is that right?"

"That's right."

"Up to that point, it's smooth sailing. But now we start to enter rough waters—that is, the seas of supposition. Here's how I think things went. The SUV pulls over, the guy driving gets out, gets into the backseat and pretends he's looking for something. Then he opens the door on the side nearest the crowd and asks Ninetta a question. The girl comes closer, and at that instant the bus pulls in. At that point nobody, passengers and driver included, is looking at the SUV anymore. The passengers are all pushing towards the entrance. Caruana watches them in the rearview mirror. It all takes just a few seconds, but long enough for the kidnapper."

"All right, makes sense, but how did he do it?"

"There's only one way he could have done it, by resorting to swift, sudden violence. The kidnapper grabs Ninetta by the arm, pulling her inside, while with his other hand he deals her a punch that knocks her out. He gets out of the backseat, gets back behind the wheel, and drives off. Think about it for a second, and you'll see that the whole operation may be extremely risky, but it's possible."

"You're right. . . ."

"And the way he acted adds another stroke to our portrait of the kidnapper. The guy's got an exceptionally cool head. He can calculate time to perfection, he never gets upset, knows how to exploit any situation to his advantage. And he's prepared to use violence at the drop of a hat."

"I don't understand why he would go into the backseat."

"It's a perfect example of the way his thoughts are organized. If he put her out of action in the front seat, how was he going to drive with an unconscious girl flopping all over the place? In the backseat he not only had more room to maneuver, but he can lay the girl down so that there's no interference with his driving."

"And when Ninetta comes to and tries to get up, he shoves her back down and puts her away with a few more punches," Fazio concluded.

"There you go. Which would be part of the scene that Vilardo witnessed when he was in the park."

For a few moments they both sat there in silence, each lost in his own thoughts about the reconstruction they had just made. At a certain point Fazio started shaking his head and making a doubtful face.

"What is it?"

"Chief, I think there's something in our reconstruction of the kidnapping that doesn't make sense."

"What would that be?"

"Why in all your different arguments did you never take into account the possibility that Ninetta and her kidnapper already knew each other?"

"And what would that mean?"

"First of all, that we should investigate further inside her circle of acquaintances. And second, that Ninetta may have climbed aboard the SUV of her own accord and wasn't forced."

"I am convinced that it would only be a waste of time."

"Why?"

"Because Ninetta and her kidnapper saw each other for

the first time in Via delle Rose, at the number three bus stop."

"What makes you so sure of that?"

"I'm going on what the driver of the three bus told you. When he pulls up, the SUV is stopped and is taking up part of the area reserved for the bus; it's even a bother both to the bus and the passengers, but Ninetta keeps talking to the stranger in the backseat. How long do you think it takes for the passengers to get into the already full bus? Half a minute? The SUV's still there. It leaves at almost the same moment as the bus, just a second before."

"So why does this lead you to conclude that the two didn't know each other beforehand?"

"Good God, Fazio, just think for a second! If they knew each other, the whole business wouldn't have lasted more than ten seconds. The SUV pulls up, the driver sees Ninetta standing there waiting for the bus, he opens the door, calls to Ninetta, telling her he'll give her a ride, she recognizes him and gets in in a hurry so as not to be in the bus's way, and the SUV drives off with half the passengers still waiting to board."

Fazio thought about this for a moment.

"You're right," he concluded.

Then:

"So what should I do? Go and talk to that lady?"

"I don't think she saw anything. There's no point. Instead, you should give Signor Bonmarito a ring and ask him if he has any news. You can call him from here."

But he didn't want to listen to the phone call, so he got up and went over to the window to smoke a cigarette. When he'd finished it and turned around, Fazio was setting down the receiver.

"No news. The poor guy was crying."

Montalbano made a decision.

"Listen. I think you should go see him straightaway."

"What for?"

"Have him write up a missing persons report. I think the time has come to let Bonetti-Alderighi in on this. He can organize a proper search party, whereas we're just sitting here holding class."

But he would take his time. Talking with the commissioner wasn't exactly the sort of thing that filled him with joy.

"... Yes, Mr. Commissioner, the father came in to report her disappearance. I have a well-grounded suspicion that we have a kidnapping on our hands ... No, I didn't say anything about evidence, just a suspicion ... Okay, okay, whatever you say ... Yes, right, the girl's a legal adult ... I'm well aware what the law requires, but, you see, more than forty-eight hours have gone by ... Inspector Seminara? ... Ah, you mean he'll be leading the investigation? ... No, for heaven's sake, a distinguished colleague like that, brilliant, in fact ... No, never fear, no interference on my part ... Furthest thing from my mind ... My best regards, sir ..."

He called Catarella.

"Is Fazio back?"

"'E jess got back now."

"Tell him to come to my office."

Fazio came in with a face so sad he looked like his dog had just died.

"What's wrong?"

"Chief, just spending fifteen minutes with the Bonmaritos breaks my heart. The wife's laid up in bed and can't move, and the guy's no longer right in the head. So sad!"

"Did you get the report?"

"Yessir."

"Good. Ring the commissioner's office, ask for Inspector Seminara, and tell him the whole story."

"Inspector Seminara? Why?"

"Because as of this moment he's the one officially leading the investigation into the kidnapping. Our commissioner's given us the boot."

"Why?"

"Jeez, is that all you can say, why? I feel like I'm in a kindergarten! There may be any number of reasons. First of all, the guy doesn't think I'm equal to the task. Second, Seminara is Calabrian."

"So? What's that got to do with anything?"

"Bonetti-Alderighi is firmly convinced that Calabrians are better equipped to understand kidnappings than other people. Don't you remember he did the exact same thing a few years ago when that other girl was kidnapped?"

"You're right."

"Come on, stop making that face!"

"I'm really sorry we have to wash our hands of this, Chief. And if I may say so, I'm also pretty surprised you didn't put up a fight and dig in."

"Who ever said we're not going to be working on the case anymore?"

Fazio gave him a baffled look.

"You did. If Inspector Seminara's supposed to take over, obviously we're—"

"So what? He'll be handling it officially, and we'll stay on the case without telling anyone."

Fazio's eyes sparkled with contentment.

"Anyway," the inspector concluded, "I'm convinced that Seminara, who's no fool, will end up asking us to work with him."

And, indeed, less than fifteen minutes later:

"Ahh Chief! 'Ere'd be a 'Sspector Seminata onna line sez he's a collie o' yiz in Montelusa."

"Ciao, Montalbano."

"Ciao, Seminara."

"Nice little hassle the commissioner's thrown in my lap! Sorry, but I have to obey orders. Your man Fazio told me you guys'd already started moving on this. It would be a big help to me if you could tell me how far you've gone with it. As long as you've got no objections, of course."

He talked like he was walking on eggshells, being well aware of the prickly character of his *collie* Montalbano.

"Come on over whenever you like."

"How about tomorrow morning around ten?" Seminara asked, reassured.

"All right."

"Oh, and listen: Fazio told me the girl's family is really poor and you think the motive for the kidnapping was sexual."

"We're pretty sure of it, unfortunately."

"So there'd be no point in putting a tap on the parents' phone?"

"I really don't think so."

15

He went out to eat.

Despite the fact that Hizzoner the C'mishner had, as they say, taken him off the case, he felt neither angry nor disappointed. Maybe because Seminara was a solid person, conscientious and stubborn. A good hunting dog who would certainly confront Ninetta's kidnapping head-on.

And the most important thing was to free the girl as quickly as possible, if she was still alive. But he was having rather grave doubts that Ninetta was indeed still alive.

As soon as he sat down at the usual table, Enzo came up to him with an envelope in his hand.

"This came for you about ten minutes ago."

Well, well! He'd gotten in touch! It was the usual envelope addressed to him, with the words *Treasure Hunt*.

"Who brought it?"

"A little kid who ran away as soon as he delivered it."

The exact same method as when the package with the lamb's head was delivered. Probably a child picked off the street, given the envelope or parcel, told where to take it, awarded a euro for a tip, with the recommendation to run away as soon as he's made the delivery. Try and find him!

He stuck the envelope in his jacket pocket. His challenger could wait. The guy was taking his time, so the inspector could do the same.

"What have you got for me?"

"Whatever you want."

"Well, I want everything."

"Got a good appetite today?"

"Not really. But if I can just pick at a little of everything, in the end I will have eaten despite the fact that I'm not hungry."

He ended up stuffing himself just the same. And for the first time in his life, he felt ashamed.

Then, while heading towards the jetty, he asked himself why he should feel ashamed for overeating.

It was, of course, specifically because of Ninetta's kidnapping. What? The wretched girl, at that very moment, is being subjected to God knows what sorts of torments at the hands of a captor taking brutal advantage of her, and the inspector on the case, the man who's supposed to liberate her, goes and gorges himself to his heart's content, not giving a flying fuck about her and her predicament?

Wait a minute, Montalbà, don't start spouting bullshit. Take, for example, a case where some of the rescue workers trying to help someone buried under the rubble of a house after an earthquake, who hasn't had a bite to eat or a drop to drink for three days, decide, out of solidarity and compassion for the victim, not to eat or drink for three days. What happens? Well, after three days of privation, they no longer have the strength to rescue the guy buried under the rubble.

Ergo, the more they eat, the better shape they're in for their rescue work.

Ergo, my ass, said Montalbano Two. *It's one thing to eat the right amount, and another thing to gorge yourself the way you do.*

Tell me the difference.

Eating is a duty, gorging yourself is a pleasure.

You're wrong there. Let me ask you a question. Why, in your opinion, do I eat so much?

Because you're someone who can't control himself.

Wrong. I could be hungry as a wolf, but if I'm caught up in a case I'm able to go whole days without eating. Therefore, when I have to, I can control myself.

Well, then you tell me why you eat so much.

I could reply that it has something to do with my metabolism, since by eating in this fashion I really should gain weight, and yet my weight stays always more or less the same, except when I'm doing nothing, which was the case until a few days ago. And I never even have liver trouble. The truth of the matter is something a friend once told me. Which was that for me, eating is a sort of accelerator of my brain function. Simple as that. So knock it off with all this shame and remorse.

He took his stroll out to the lighthouse very slowly, one foot up, the other foot down. Because, if there was no question but that food lubricated his brain, it was also true that it slowed down his pace.

When he reached the flat rock, he sat down and smoked a cigarette in peace.

Then he started pestering a crab, throwing little pebbles at it. At last he decided to take out the envelope, open it, and read what was inside.

I beg your pardon, dear policeman,
but your wait, you'll see, does have its reason.

Day and night, my work and pleasure
is all to enrich your hunt for the treasure.

My next task truly makes me tremble:
to change real to real that it resemble.

Trust me: when you at last the answer reap,
real tears of joy your eyes will weep.

Await my next move; this you can handle,
for the game is worth more than the candle.

Huh? The prankster really could have spared himself the trouble of writing these lines, which hobbled worse than an unlucky cripple.

What, in essence, did they say?

That he had to wait because the guy was working hard to make the treasure better. Well, good luck.

There was probably no point in showing the poem to Arturo, so useless did it seem. Then he thought about it and decided that it wouldn't be right. He'd promised the kid, who was supposed to be his teammate, and he had to make good on his promise and keep the kid informed of any new developments. But he didn't feel like seeing him. The youth, with his Harry Potterish whiz-kid airs, was starting to get on his nerves. He reread the poem, and this time he began to get worried. There was something ugly in those lines. And what was he to make of that third couplet?

"Any sign of Inspector Augello?"

"Nossir, Chief."

What the hell had happened to him?

"Any phone calls?"

"Jess one, Chief. 'At kid 'oo's a frenna Signura Scioscio-strommi's . . ."

What was little Master Arturo trying to do? Become a pain in the ass? A phone call a day? This time, however, the timing was right.

"Did he leave a phone number?"

"Yessir, sir."

"Give him a ring and tell him to come here to the station to pick up an envelope I've got for him."

He pulled it out of his pocket, handed it to Catarella, and went into his office.

He hadn't even had time to sit down when a blast in the

decibel range of a cherry bomb exploded behind him, making him leap forward to the point where he very nearly crashed his head against the wall.

"Beckin' y' partin', Chief," said Catarella in the doorway. "My 'and slipped."

"You'd better watch out, Cat, 'cause one of these days my hand is gonna slip, too, and it's not gonna be pretty for you."

Catarella fell silent, staring at his shoe tops as if humiliated.

"What do you want?"

"Ya gotta 'scuse me, Chief, I tink ya got the wrong invilope," he said, handing him the same envelope he'd given him moments before.

Montalbano took it and looked at it to make sure. It was in fact the one for the treasure hunt.

"Why do you think it's the wrong one?"

"Insomuch as 'ere iss writ sayin' as how the litter's f'yiz, meanin' yiz, Isspecter Salvo Montalbano, meanin' yiz poissonally in poisson."

"So what?"

"If isstead iss from yiz, sint by yiz, I mean 'at y'wannit a sind it on yer bahaff to him, then i'oughter had writ on it 'at iss addressed to the kid 'at Signura Sciosciostrommi sint t'yiz."

What to do? Grab him and smash his head against the wall? Or else suck it up and be patient? It was better not to spill any blood.

"You're right, Cat. The letter's addressed to me, but I want the kid to read it too."

Catarella's doubtful face cheered up. As he headed for the door, Montalbano looked down at a sheet of paper, but then noticed that Catarella had stopped in the doorway.

"Did your batteries go dead, Cat?"

"Wha' ba'aries, Chief?"

"Never mind. What's wrong?"

"I jess tought a sum'n. C'n I ass anutter quession?"

"Go ahead."

"If the kid wantsa talk t'yiz, whaddo I do? Put 'im true or no?"

"I don't feel like talking to him. Tell him I'm in a meeting."

Augello showed up as it was getting dark.

"You really took your time, Mimì."

"I did not take my time," Mimì retorted, sitting down. "I wasted the whole day chasing down Alba."

"And who's that?"

"Alba Giordano. Professionally she goes by Samantha. The girl from the brothel."

"Did you talk to her?"

"Yes, but the whole thing was incredibly long and drawn out. When I got to the address I had for her in Vincinzella, I knocked and knocked but nobody answered. Then a neighbor lady said that the Giordanos had moved to Ragona a couple of weeks ago. And since they'd given her the new address, I headed off to Ragona. I located the house, but then I had a problem."

"What do you mean?"

"What was I supposed to do? Introduce myself to her mother and father?"

"Wasn't that the most logical thing?"

"No."

"Why not?"

"What if they didn't know the first thing about what their daughter was doing with her free time?"

"But hadn't Alba been identified? Is it possible her parents knew nothing about it?"

"And what if the father knew and the mother didn't? Or vice versa? I would have created a big mess."

"Your scruples do you honor, Inspector Augello. Your profound humanity, your exquisite sensitivity—"

"Fuck off."

"So what did you do?"

"I went to the carabinieri."

Montalbano balked and goggled his eyes. He literally leapt up in his chair.

"The carabinieri? Are you crazy?"

"No. Why, have they got the mange or something?"

"That's not what I meant, but—"

"Salvo, I had nowhere else to go. There wasn't any local police station. I thought about it a long time before going to them."

"And did you tell them who you were?"

"Of course."

"And wha'd they do?"

"What do you think? That they kicked me out? The marshal was extremely polite and put himself entirely at my disposal. And you know what? The guy's got a mind just like Fazio's. He knows everything about every inhabitant of Ragona from cradle to grave."

"So wha'd you tell him?"

"The truth."

"What part?"

Mimì looked puzzled.

"I don't understand."

"Did you tell him the whole truth, from the very beginning, or did you only sing half the Mass?"

"I still don't understand."

"I'll speak more clearly. Did you tell this marshal of the carabinieri—now pay close attention—that you first saw Alba in a photo album at a 'house of assignation' where you'd gone as a client?"

Mimì first turned bright red, then pale as a corpse. He was about to get up and leave without a word, but then managed to control himself. He swallowed two or three times, ran a hand over his lips, and then said in a slightly quavering voice:

"No, I didn't think it was important."

"Why not?"

"Because it had nothing to do with what I had to ask him."

"It didn't?"

"No, it didn't."

"Tell me something. Did the marshal tell you how Alba behaves when she's in Ragona?"

"Yes, he said her conduct is irreproachable."

"And did you tell him that in fact she occasionally works as a prostitute?"

"I couldn't help but do so."

"And how'd he react?"

"He was very surprised."

"Only surprised?"

"He said that from now on he would keep an eye on her."

"All right. This is where I wanted to take you. The honest public servant of the police didn't hesitate to let the carabinieri know that Alba had worked as a prostitute, neglecting, however, to say that he himself had wanted to be a client of hers. That's all. You were able to leave looking as clean as when you arrived, whereas she's now branded as a whore."

"But it was you yourself who gave me the assignment to go and look for her, to make her talk and—"

"The assignment I gave you was to go and meet with her alone, without involving anyone else. In fact I even asked you to resort to your well-known arts as a seducer. And this, indirectly, meant that you shouldn't involve the carabinieri, the customs police, or the forest rangers."

Mimì remained silent for a moment. Then he said:

"You're right."

"That's all. Go on."

"The marshal agreed with me that it was rather unlikely the parents knew anything about the life their daughter led. Since Alba'd had an accident on her moped the day before, he had a carabiniere summon her using that as an excuse. When the girl came in they led her into the room that the marshal had made available to me."

"Wait a second. Why did she move to Ragona?"

"Because her father wanted to take her away from the crowd she was running with and managed to get a work transfer and brought the family along."

"So what did she say to you?"

"Well, let me start by saying that she's an exceptional girl."

"You'd already s—"

"I wasn't referring to her beauty, Salvo. She was exceptional in the way she spoke to me about what she did. She was perfectly natural, as if she was talking about working as a salesgirl. She didn't regret it and she wasn't proud of it, either. Since she was the pride of the house—those were her exact words—the madam would use her to attract new clients by word of mouth and then arrange it so that she didn't have any regular clients."

"So, at any rate, was it all a waste of time?"

"Basically, yes. But she did tell me something. She could only stay at the house for an hour at a time."

"How did she get there?"

"On her motorbike. She would tell her parents she was going to see a friend, or to the movies, or the library. . . ."

"Go on."

"One day, when she'd finished her hour and was about to leave to go home, the madam told her to be careful. And she explained that in the past few days a client had asked for her twice, and she'd told him she wasn't available."

"So what was the problem?"

"She said the guy seemed like a loose cannon. The first time he saw her photo he'd got so excited that he actually started to tremble. The madam got scared. And since that day he'd come back three times and got pretty upset that Alba was never available, the madam thought he might be lurking somewhere in the area, waiting for her to come out. So Alba decided to stay at the house for a few more hours. She phoned her mother to let her know and invented an excuse for being late. When she finally left to go home, it was after eight and already dark. When she drove past the Sammartino bridge, where on the right-hand side there are some woods, a car that had been following her ran her off the road."

"Did she see what kind of car it was?"

"No, she never even thought about it. She was too scared. As she was getting up—she'd hardly hurt herself at all—she saw the guy get out of the car and come running towards her. She was so paralyzed by fear that she couldn't move."

"Is she sure the guy did it on purpose?"

"Absolutely certain. Luckily at that moment another car came by and pulled over. So the guy who'd caused the accident turned tail and ran back to his car, got in, and drove off in a hurry."

"I think that tells us the driver was the unhappy client."

"Of course. In my opinion, if the other car hadn't arrived, he would have dragged her off into the woods and raped her."

"So Alba didn't get a good look at his face?"

"No."

"And did he turn up again any time after that?"

"Well, three days later, our colleagues from Montelusa raided the place."

"Do you know what this means, Mimì?"

"Yes, that I have to track down the madam and get her to describe the client who wanted Alba."

"Right. I'll go and see Zurlo first thing tomorrow morning. You said they arrested her, no? So, even if she's out, they'll certainly know where she lives. But we don't have a minute to lose, Mimì, I mean it."

"I know," said Augello, getting up.

"Ah, listen Mimì, I almost forgot. I wanted to let you know that the case isn't ours anymore."

Augello, who had already stood up, sat back down.

"I don't understand."

"What's to understand? Bonetti-Alderighi snatched it away from us and gave it to Seminara."

"Why on earth?"

"Because Seminara is Calabrian, and we're not up to the task."

"So what am I doing going to see the madam?"

"Just go anyway, because Seminara wants us to work with him. So we're authorized to conduct a parallel investigation."

"Do you think that's really what Seminara meant?"

"No, but that's my interpretation, all right? Don't you agree?"

"Me?! Absolutely!"

"So go and get the madam to tell you everything we want to know, and then we'll decide together whether or not we should report it to Seminara. Get my drift?"

"Got it."

Ten minutes later, as he was leaving the office, Catarella called to him.

"Ah, Chief. Yer litter."

And he held out the treasure-hunt envelope.

"Just keep it. If the kid hasn't come by yet, you'll see that—"

"Nah, Chief, the kid come by awright, an' he copied it down an' give it back to me. 'E even left a missage."

A page from Catarella's notebook.

Dear Inspector

Just a few lines to tell you my immediate impression after a hasty reading of the new letter. Though I couldn't explain rationally why, it seemed very disturbing to me.

Especially the line that says "real tears of joy your eyes will weep." It's the choice of the verb here that seems strange to me. Though it does happen sometimes, joy is not usually the reason we weep. Joy usually makes us smile or laugh. But I get the feeling that's not the case here.

And then the writer seems so keen to let us know he's working day and night to make the treasure unique and unrepeatable . . . I repeat, it's only an impression, but I fear that when we find the treasure we're going to be in for a nasty surprise. Please keep me informed.

> *Cordially yours,*
> *Arturo*

16

He put the piece of paper in his pocket and headed home.

Hats off to Arturo, anyway, since when he'd first finished reading the note himself, sitting under the lighthouse, he'd had the same feeling of unease. But he'd chosen not to analyze it; it would have taken his thoughts off Ninetta. Now that Arturo had brought it up again, however, the feeling was back. It was true: there was something vaguely menacing about those words.

But all he could do was take note of this, since no initiative was possible at the moment.

Sitting out on the veranda after eating, he was thinking about when and how Ninetta's kidnapper might come out of the woodwork, and the only possible scenario spinning around in his head was, unfortunately, that in the next few days someone would call in to say that they'd found the corpse of a young woman in a dump or under a bridge. Then suddenly, under its own power, for no explicable reason, another idea elbowed its way into his mind, pushing aside the image of Ninetta's dead body and moving squarely into the forefront of his brain.

He got up, went inside, pulled the treasure-hunt message out of his jacket pocket, grabbed all the other messages he'd received earlier, including Arturo's note, and went back out on the veranda, spread them all out on the table, one letter after another, sat back down, and reread them all. And then he did it again.

And little by little, as he was reading and rereading them, and remembering how and when he'd received them, the streets and paths they'd sent him on, the places they'd led him, the wooden hut, the ruined house, the furrow in the middle of his brow grew deeper and deeper.

But the idea was so loopy, so off-the-wall, so lacking in any solid foundation that he was afraid to formulate it in full, to give it a definitive shape and thereby force himself to consider it as a whole.

So he just let it float freely in his brain, in scraps and bits, cuts and details, like the pieces of a puzzle, and he kept going over and over these fragments, but in such a way that they continued to remain separate from one another, because once they began to come together and form a coherent picture, he would be forced to take action, to get moving, with the risk, however, that in the end it would all turn out to have been a game, something to pass the time, and on it he would have staked not only his reputation and career—which he really didn't give a damn about—but also his self-esteem and self-image. No, the more he thought it through, the more he considered it from all sides, the more convinced he became that the treasure hunt was not at all an innocent game, but something decidedly dangerous. Not only did it smell of blood (the lamb's head was certainly proof of that), but there was a stench of rot, of decaying flesh, of sickness, around the whole affair.

If things were really the way he was seeing them now, then ever since the first letter, the prize the challenger was dangling as a reward had to be something hair-raising, and he should have realized this from the start.

Worse yet, he'd taken it as a silly game, an amusement, a prank, and therefore had not given enough weight to all the things his adversary had tried to tell him between the lines.

But what was all this conjecture based on? On words alone.

Not only, but on a personal interpretation of a small handful of words. Were they enough to justify forming so fanciful a hypothesis?

"Let us base our actions on facts."

This was what his boss, the man who'd taught him the secrets of the trade when he was a deputy inspector, always used to say at the start of an investigation.

"It's facts that matter, Salvo, not words."

But what if words helped you to understand the facts? Might it not be better, in that case, to consider words first?

And how many times in the past had a word that was said or not said put him on the right track? How did the Latin saying go? *Ex ore tuo te judico.* But even assuming that it was possible to judge someone by his words, the real problem still lay in a question that was at the bottom of all his doubts: Couldn't the interpretation he was giving the whole thing be completely wrong?

Maybe if he discussed it with Arturo . . . but the guy would just take to it like gangbusters and start splitting hairs like nobody's business. . . . No, at this point it was best not to expose himself, not say anything to him about this new idea, which was too wild, too unfounded. . . . The kid might start to think he was getting senile.

But what if the idea turned out to be right? Wouldn't he, Montalbano, have a terrible weight forever on his conscience, for not having acted in time? In time? Act? But how?

All he had in his head was a conjecture, a hunch, of a possible connection within a handful of words. But, even if he managed to persuade himself to do something, what exactly was it he was supposed to do?

And even this, if he really thought about it, wasn't true.

Because he knew perfectly well what he had to do to have at least some kind of proof that his conjecture wasn't mistaken. He just didn't have the courage to do it.

Want to bet that this lack of courage was nothing more than an effect of aging? That's what people are like when they get old; they become excessively prudent.

How did the saying go? We're born arsonists and we die firemen.

No! Aging didn't have a damn thing to do with this! It was simply a matter of not making a mistake out of an excess of what one might call youthful enthusiasm over an idea without foundation.

Oh, yeah? So words don't, after all, constitute a foundation? And what is human civilization founded on if not words? And what are we to make of *In the beginning was the Word*?

Stop, Montalbà, come back down to earth. Where are your cogitations taking you? Can't you see that you're so tired you're starting to talk nonsense?

In the beginning was the word! Give me a break! I think it's a better idea if you just go to bed!

He gathered together the pieces of paper, locked the French door, and got into bed.

But he didn't sleep a wink. He was too afraid that while he slept, against his will, the pieces of the puzzle might come together, treacherously, each in its proper place.

———

It wasn't even seven in the morning when the phone started ringing.

Completely numbed from his bad night, he dragged himself out of bed and headed for the dining room, banging against everything it was possible to bang against, chairs, corners, doors. He was walking exactly like a sleepwalker.

"Hello?"

But his voice came out so clotted and incomprehensible that Catarella said:

"Beckin' y'partin', I got da wrong nummer."

And he hung up. Montalbano turned around and took two steps back towards the bedroom when the phone rang again. At the first ring, as though ordered by a drill sergeant, he turned on his heels, did an about-face, and grabbed the receiver. He was in an utter daze. He cleared his throat.

"Hello."

"Ahh Chief! Ahh Chief, Chief!"

Bad sign. Normally Catarella began a phone call in this fashion either when Hizzoner the C'mishner wanted him or as a solemn prelude to the announcement of a little murder.

"What is it?"

"A 'Murcan gurl jess called."

"But do you speak American?"

"Nah, Chief, but I know a coupla woids 'cause I gotta a sister-in-laws 'ass a 'Murcan, 'nso now 'n' 'enn . . ."

"What did she want?"

"She's rilly rilly upsett an' scared, Chief! An' she's yellin' into the phone o'the receiver! 'N so, also 'cause she's so scared 'n upsett, I din't unnastan' too much."

"What did you manage to understand?"

"A' foist she started repittin' a same ting, kindalike deedee deedee . . ."

"And what does that mean?"

"Chief, in a 'Murcan spitch deedee means cadaffer."

"Is that all she said?"

"No, Chief, 'enn she startet sayin' lecky lecky."

"Which means?"

"In a 'Murcan spitch lecky means lake."

The electrical shock that rattled the inspector's body from his brain to the tips of his toes was almost painful.

"And then?"

"Ann'enn nuttin'. She 'ung up."

"Fazio there?"

"'E in't onna premises yet."

"How about Gallo?"

"Yessir."

"Tell him to come and get me at once."

The fog that had been clouding his brain was suddenly gone, as if blown away by a gust of wind. He was perfectly lucid.

Because he knew, unfortunately, that his hunch was soon to become a certainty. All the pieces of the puzzle that he'd been trying to keep far apart from each other all through the night were now, after that phone call, fitting snugly into their assigned places.

He didn't have the time to take a shower or shave, but managed to wash up a little and drink four cups of coffee in a row before Gallo arrived.

"What's this about, Chief?"

"The last stage of a treasure hunt."

It was the inspector's tone that made Gallo realize that it wasn't the time to ask any other questions on the subject.

"Where do you want me to take you?"

"I want you to take the road to Gallotta, and just before the town, there's a little dirt road with a sign on the left for a wine tavern. You have to turn down that road and stop in front of the tavern. You can go as fast as you like, and don't forget to turn on the siren."

Gallo looked at him in astonishment and was off like a rocket.

Montalbano closed his eyes and put himself in God's hands.

———

"Now turn off the siren and try to make as little noise as possible," Montalbano said as soon as they turned onto the narrow dirt path between the trees that led to the tavern.

The little house's doors and windows were still closed. So much the better. The inspector didn't want any curious busybodies following after them.

"Now what?"

"Now pay attention. Keep going straight, but you'll soon find yourself on a treacherous trail that only four-by-fours can handle. Think you can manage it?"

By way of reply, Gallo grinned and started driving without making the slightest noise. He really was good.

At moments the inspector was afraid the car would flip over or fall onto its side with its wheels in the air, but Gallo was able to hold the road. When they reached the shore of the lake, however, he was drenched in sweat.

"Now what?"

"I'm getting out to smoke a cigarette, you can do whatever you like."

He didn't really feel like smoking a cigarette, it was just an excuse to delay the moment of truth a little longer. Or perhaps to get his mind ready for what he was about to see— or, more precisely, what he would have to endure, if what he'd imagined turned out to be right.

Because what he'd imagined was horror. Sheer horror.

A horror that was sure to seem all the more unbearable on that perfect morning, with the air so crisp it made the colors sharp as knives, and the lake water really did look like a piece of the sky that had fallen to earth. All perfectly still. Not a blade of grass moving. Total silence. No birds singing or dogs barking in the distance. A calm before a storm would have caused less anguish.

Usually he smoked his cigarettes three-quarters down, but this time he didn't toss it to the ground until it was burning his fingers. And he wasted still more time carefully snuffing it out with his heel.

He got back into the car. Gallo had remained inside, slightly spooked by the inspector's behavior.

"See that little house?"

"Yeah?"

"Think you could make it up there?"

"Piece of cake."

The inspector simply didn't feel like going up that little stretch of inclined road on foot. His legs were already too wobbly.

"Now what?" asked Gallo, pulling up right in front of the missing door.

Jeez, what a pain in the ass with this *Now what* crap!

"Now we go inside. I'll go first and you follow."

"Isn't it better if I go first?"

"Why?"

"What if there's someone who—"

"There's nobody. If only there *were* somebody to start shooting at us!"

"What's that supposed to mean, Chief?" Gallo asked, stunned.

"It means I would prefer that."

And he opened the door to step out. But Gallo held him back, putting one hand on his arm.

"What's in there, Chief?"

"If it's what I think, it's something so horrific that it'll haunt your dreams for the rest of your life. If you want, you can stay in the car."

"I don't think so," said Gallo, getting out.

Despite the fact that he'd prepared himself as best he could, gritting his teeth as he climbed the unsteady wooden stairs, what he saw stopped him dead in his tracks and knocked the wind out of him.

Coming up behind him, Gallo, as soon as he saw the thing lying on the floor in the middle of the room, froze for a second or two, then let out a cry of fear, so shrill it sounded like a woman's, turned around, put one foot on the staircase, stumbled down to the third step, fell to the ground, got up, ran out of the house, and started throwing up his soul, letting out a continuous wail like a wild animal.

A few minutes later, Montalbano came out of the house. He'd succeeded in regaining his self-control and forcing his eyes to look at the thing.

My next task truly makes me tremble:
to change real to real that it resemble.

Because the nude body was indeed Ninetta's, there was no doubt about that. But her body had been changed into that of an inflatable doll, exactly like the other two.

The killer had gouged out one of her eyes, torn out clumps of hair, and punctured the body repeatedly, covering the holes with adhesive bandages. . . .

But the most horrifying thing was that he'd painted her lips red with lipstick, redrawn her eyebrows with eyebrow pencil, spread a bit of rouge over her cheekbones . . . And to lend color to her body he had smeared makeup foundation all over it. Death had stamped a sort of grimace on Ninetta's face, leaving the teeth bared. A terrifying mask, precisely because it was at once real and fake.

So he really must have worked very hard to "enrich" the hunt and its treasure, the grand prize. But the inspector wasn't at all happy about winning the challenge. On the contrary, he would rather have lost it a million times over.

Coming out of the house, he wondered for a moment whether he should go over to the woods where Fazio said a group of young foreigners had pitched camp. It must have been a girl from their group who'd found the corpse and called the police. But then he realized he wouldn't find anyone there; they must surely all have run away.

He went and sat down on a rock beside Gallo, who for his part was sitting on the ground, face buried in his hands.

"Why?" he asked the inspector almost voicelessly.

"Is there a reason for madness?"

"Look, I'm not going back in there."

"You don't have to. We're going to get back in the car now and call Fazio. He knows this place. All he has to do is inform Inspector Seminara that we've found Ninetta's body."

When they'd done this, Gallo's inevitable question came.

"Now what?"

"Let's get out of here. We'll go back to the lake."

This time Gallo drove so poorly that the car very nearly rolled down the slope and crashed.

"Now what?"

"Feel up to standing guard here?"

"Sure. What about you?"

"I'd rather not be here when they arrive. Just tell Seminara to ring me whenever he wants."

He got out of the car and headed towards the dirt road. Better that path, which looked like some infernal landscape out of Doré, than stay a second longer back there, amidst all that beauty infected with violence, cruelty, and madness.

He reached the tavern about half an hour later, dead tired from the walk. Luckily the place was open and the woman sitting in her usual chair, peeling potatoes.

"Wha' c'n I git for you?"

"Half a liter."

At the bar she put a bottle with the liquid volume measured down to the milliliter in front of him, along with a glass.

"Do you know whether there are any taxis in Gallotta?"

"No sir, but my son's got a car."

"Is he here?"

"No sir, in Gallotta."

"Could you call him and ask if he could drive me to Vigàta?"

"Yessir."

He grabbed a chair, went and sat outside, filled his glass, and set the bottle down on the ground.

It was truly a glorious morning. The air was clean and fine, and everything gleamed as if it had just been polished. It looked like the first day of creation. But perhaps that was why it was so unbearable to him that he had to drown it in wine. Beautiful forms often make horror more salient.

"He'll be here in about twenty minutes," said the old woman.

There was only one good side to what had happened—if you really could call it good. And that was that he wouldn't have to be the one to tell the poor Bonmaritos that their daughter had been murdered.

Mimì came in around noon, but he already knew about the discovery of the body because Fazio had phoned him.

"Did you find the madam?"

"Yes. She's at home, on house arrest. She lives in Campobello."

"What did she tell you?"

"She only gave me general sort of information. I don't know if it's because she's got a bad memory for faces or just afraid to talk. All she said was that the guy was young, dark, rather tall, and well dressed."

"If we showed him to her, would she recognize him?"

"She said maybe yes. But I wouldn't trust her. She might see him and recognize him and then turn around and tell us it's not him."

"So you think it's best to forget about her?"

"I'd say so."

Gallo got back past one.

"Jesus, what a morning, Chief! First it was Prosecutor Tommaseo, who got it in his head to come in his own car. At the start of the dirt road leading to the lake, he drove into a ditch and we had to pull him out with chains; then the ambulance couldn't make it either, and they had to carry the body on foot all the way to the tavern. . . ."

"Did Pasquano come?"

"Of course."

"What did he say?"

"Just that the girl hadn't been killed there. Nothing else."

There was no need for all of Dr. Pasquano's knowledge to figure that out.

17

He got a ride home to Marinella. Then he unplugged the phone and went to bed. An hour later, he woke up, took a long shower, and went and sat down on the veranda.

And, like the previous evening, he spread out across the table the murderer's letters and the note from Arturo.

Words, words, words, as Mina used to sing in the song.

What new things could these words tell him that they hadn't already? It was thanks to his ability to interpret them that he'd suddenly known where to find Ninetta's body. Nevertheless, he had an obscure feeling that these words could still reveal a number of things to him. He had to steel his patience and keep reading and rereading them, maybe breaking them down, syllable by syllable, paying close attention to periods and commas . . .

But wouldn't it be better to ask Arturo to help? The kid was a student of words. Philosophy is made up of words; the boy could grasp the sense, meaning, weight, and texture of every word. Yes, it was the only way.

Montalbano got up, went inside, sat down by the phone, and was about to pick up the receiver when he froze.

Arturo.

A violent flash of light blinded him for a moment, but illuminated his brain. A trickle of sweat rolled down from his head, under his shirt, and gave him a cold shudder. Yes, he was in a cold sweat.

Arturo.

He ran back outside, picked up the last message and Arturo's note and placed them side by side. An obvious discrepancy jumped out at him.

The insane murderer—he didn't feel like calling him a "prankster" or "challenger" anymore, so much had things changed—had written:

Day and night, my work and pleasure
is all to enrich your hunt for the treasure.

Whereas in his note Arturo had changed the second line to "make the treasure unique and unrepeatable."

Wasn't the long, horrific, painstaking work done on poor Ninetta's body better described by Arturo's words than by those of the killer himself?

"Unique and unrepeatable" were much more precise, better cut to measure than "enrich your hunt," which was rather general and could refer to just about any outcome. Whereas those used by the kid fitted so perfectly as to seem the only ones possible.

But how could Arturo have been in a position to foresee the uniqueness and unrepeatability of that crime?

There was only one explanation possible, which was that the kid already knew what the killer would do to poor Ninetta's body. And the only person who could have known this was the killer himself.

Or an accomplice of his.

No, wrong. No accomplices. Wasn't it Arturo himself who told him that the treasure hunt was less a game than a duel, a challenge to the death between two people? That was why he made the slip.

More importantly, however, instead of dwelling, in his note, on the tears of joy, why hadn't he mentioned the two lines that were the most incomprehensible of all and had so upset the inspector when he first read them on the rock by the sea?

My next task truly makes me tremble:
to change real to real that it resemble.

An unconscious slip and a willful omission. Willful in order to distract attention away from his main intention: to transform a human body into an inflatable rubber doll.

A slip and omission that were bigger than a house.

By this point he was so drenched in sweat that he had to go back inside and take another shower. As the water was washing over his body and refreshing him, he began to review every encounter he'd had with Arturo, trying to remember every word they'd said to each other.

So, during their first meeting, the kid had said he'd wanted to meet him to understand how his brain functioned during an investigation.

Wasn't it possible that Arturo, in challenging him with the treasure hunt, had in reality wanted to assign the investigation a theme? By forcing him down a predetermined path, the kid would know how things would unfold; and if he already knew all the details in advance, wouldn't that make it easier for him to follow the functioning of the inspector's brain? And to be doubly sure, the kid had even had the cheek to introduce himself to him and get himself accepted as the inspector's advisor.

Extremely dangerous. This was a criminal mind the likes of which he had never encountered before. Arturo had preplanned everything he intended to do, down to the finest details, and then executed it without ever missing a step. So he needed an SUV to take the girl's body to the tumbledown house by way of that treacherous road? He'd stolen the car he wanted even before he had the victim in his hands. And how skillful and coldly lucid he'd been in kidnapping Ninetta on a busy street, before the eyes of so many witnesses!

In the inspector's second meeting with the youth, there were at least two things that didn't make sense. Or that made all too much sense, depending on your point of view.

The first was that when he'd asked Arturo how he'd found Via dei Mille, the kid had replied that he'd got a street guide from city hall. Which couldn't have been true since city hall didn't have street guides.

The second thing was that when he'd asked Arturo whether all the photos in the shack were still hanging on the walls, he'd said yes, they were all still there. Whereas in fact not only had Montalbano taken one, but a few others had fallen onto the floor. So the kid hadn't gone into the house, as he had claimed, because he already knew perfectly well that it was full of those photographs, since he'd put them there himself.

Then later, he'd been so insistent that Montalbano should go to the house by the lake! What had he said? Ah, yes, that there might be something inside that would prove useful to him.

And there was another omission, too. He hadn't asked the inspector how he'd come by the letter that led him to the house. This was the letter that had come in the parcel with the lamb's head. Why hadn't Arturo been curious enough to ask?

Suddenly the water stopped coming down from the tanks. Luckily Montalbano hadn't had a trace of soap on his body for quite some time. As he was getting dressed again, he had to admit to himself that all he'd been doing so far was just talk, hot air. His line of reasoning made sense, no doubt about it, but it had one flaw: it rested on the wispiest of threads, no more substantial than a spider's.

This time his interpretation of what Arturo had or hadn't said was like a rubber band stretched to the maximum and about to break at any moment.

If you really thought about it, those same words could be interpreted in the exact opposite way, which would lead to the conclusion that Arturo was not behind the treasure hunt and therefore not the killer.

No, this time, words were not enough. He imagined his conversation with Prosecutor Tommaseo.

"But what does your sense of his guilt rest on?"

"On a slip of the tongue and two omissions."

Tommaseo was sure to send for the men in white coats.

Proof was what was needed, and the inspector didn't have so much as a shadow of proof in hand. He suddenly felt disheartened. Wouldn't it be better just to forget about it all? What was the use, after all? The fact was, Ninetta was already dead and they hadn't been able to save her. He would talk to Seminara, tell him his suspicions and then let him decide.

No, he was making a mistake. He was giving up. Hadn't Arturo convinced him that this was a duel? Well, then, a duel it would be. To the death.

Anyway, he couldn't very well let a murderous madman like that run free.

But what to do?

All at once he remembered something that Donald

Rumsfeld, Bush's defense secretary, had said, when the chief of the UN inspectors sent to Iraq in search of weapons of mass destruction reported that they hadn't found a fucking thing. He'd said: "Absence of evidence is not evidence of absence." Brilliant.

And so he resolved to carry on playing the game. But no longer Arturo's game, the treasure hunt, but a game of his own choosing, which he called the game of truth. And he was sure he would win.

He glanced at his watch. Four o'clock. He dashed into the dining room and dialed Ingrid's number. He prayed to the Good Lord, or whoever was standing in for him, that he'd find her at home.

"Hello, who is this?"

He very nearly had a heart attack. How could this person be answering in perfect Italian?

"Montalbano here. I'd like to speak with Signora Ingrid, please."

"I'll put her on."

A distant murmur of voices, clicking heels drawing near.

"Ciao, Salvo, how are you?"

"I'm fine, thanks. How'd you end up with an Italian manservant?"

"Manservant? That's my husband."

Montalbano shuddered.

"Oh . . . I'm so sorry, I really didn't . . ."

"Come on! What did you want?"

"Well, I was hoping that maybe this evening you could . . ."

"But he's heading back to Rome in half an hour! Tell me, what do you want to do?"

"Can I talk?"

"What is with you?"

"Listen, you told me that Arturo was in love with you, right?"

A hearty laugh.

"Yes. More than in love. Crazy about me."

Not only about you. The guy's completely crazy, he felt like saying. But he only asked:

"Could you call him and ask him out to dinner with you tonight?"

For a moment Ingrid said nothing. Then she must have understood Montalbano's motives, but didn't ask for any explanations. She was a woman with cojones. She simply asked:

"What if he can't make it tonight?"

"Then tomorrow for lunch."

"In other words, the sooner the better."

"Yes."

"How long do you want him out of your hair?"

"A couple of hours should do."

"I'll call him right now and insist that it be tonight. Where can I reach you to let you know?"

"I'll be here at home for another ten minutes."

He hung up and called the station. As soon as he heard his voice, Catarella launched into an elaborate litany:

"Ah, Chief, Chief! Issat Isspecter Seminario, yer collie o' yers in Montelusa, whotofore's lookin' f'yiz 'n' moresomuch 'nsistn' 'e wants yiz—"

"I'm not interested. Get me Fazio."

"Straightaways, Chief."

Too bad for his *collie* Seminara, but it just wasn't the right time.

"What is it, Chief?"

"Listen, Fazio, I'm going to give you a present for you to relish to your heart's content. I want all the personal particulars of a young man of twenty, Arturo Pennisi. I also want to know where he lives in Vigàta, and anything else that might prove useful to me."

"Useful for what, Chief?"

He pretended not to have heard.

"I'll be at the station around six."

The telephone rang the moment he set down the receiver. It was Ingrid.

"It's all set for tonight. But I should warn you: I have no intention whatsoever of sleeping with him."

"I'm not asking you to."

"So you just have those two hours we'll be at the restaurant. There won't be any extensions."

"Fine, fine. What time's your appointment?"

"Eight-thirty, in front of my place."

"But can I ask a question? I'm curious."

"Go ahead."

"Why wouldn't you sleep with him?"

"Bah, I dunno, it's just an impression . . . he's certainly a nice-looking boy, very bright and all, but . . . I dunno, I have this fear . . . I think he might be a repressed sadist, actually."

Repressed, if you say so! At any rate, the upshot was that one should always trust feminine intuition.

"One last thing. When Arturo rings your buzzer outside, call me at home."

"Okay."

━━━━

"Is Dr. Pasquano in?"

"Sure, I'll let him know you're here."

Then, after ringing him, the custodian turned and said: "He's in his office."

He went down the usual long corridor and knocked on the door.

"Come in."

Pasquano was standing in front of the window, hand behind his back, contemplating the landscape. He didn't greet the inspector with the usual string of expletives he normally held in store for him. Without looking at him, he said:

"I just now finished the autopsy on that poor girl. That's what you're here for, right?"

"Yes."

Pasquano wasn't in one of his typical moods. Actually he

seemed tired and melancholy. Turning around, he went and sat down behind his desk, signaling to Montalbano to sit down as well.

"You're not in charge of the investigation."

"No."

"But you can tell me: are you conducting one on the sly?"

"Yes."

"Are you just spinning your wheels, or have you got an idea?"

"I've got one."

"Good. I really hope you catch him. I wish I could have him right here, under the knife. In all the years I've been working, I've never seen anything so horrifying . . . It's not unusual, it's . . . unique."

"And unrepeatable," said Montalbano.

"He made her look exactly like that doll that was mistaken for a corpse. He must have worked very hard at it, you know."

"I know. And the doll in the dumpster, which you saw yourself, was itself a sort of dry run, using the doll I'd found in the old man's bed as a model."

Dr. Pasquano sat there for a moment, thinking, and looking more and more melancholy. Then he said:

"I've figured it out."

"Figured what out?"

"Why he poisoned her."

"He poisoned her?"

"Yes. And I know why. He couldn't very well kill her by shooting or stabbing her. It would have left too many obvious signs on her body. Signs the model didn't have. Therefore the only way was poison. He's a subtle one, a real son of a bitch. And you know what? He poisoned her right after he kidnapped her."

"So he didn't abuse her, then."

Pasquano sneered.

"Are you kidding? Wherever and however, and repeatedly, but . . ."

It was the first time Montalbano had ever seen Pasquano so upset and shaken.

"But? . . ."

"Postmortem, know what I mean? He didn't want a living person, but an inflatable doll."

Montalbano normally thought of himself as sufficiently hardened by now, but this time he needed a couple of minutes to get over his vertigo and horror.

"I've already thrown up," Pasquano said, eyeing him. "If you feel the urge, the bathroom's the next door over. Don't be shy."

"Did he use surgical instruments to . . . ?"

"Not a chance! This was a do-it-yourself job! The eye he gouged out with a spoon, the wounds he made with an awl, for the hair he used a simple razor . . . Then he carefully bled her, spread makeup foundation all over her body, then made up her—"

"How'd he get her breast to droop?"

"He made do with some kind of home liposuction kit, which only half worked."

The doctor gazed out the window.

"And you know what else? She was a virgin. And that monster . . ."

The inspector had never heard that word before on Pasquano's lips. The doctor had never expressed personal opinions of any sort about the bodies he cut up or their killers.

". . . since he couldn't manage on his own—he must've been half impotent or something—he cleared the way with a broom handle or something similar."

He turned and looked again at Montalbano.

"Catch him. Otherwise, if he gets away, I'll bet the family jewels he'll come up with some other bright idea even worse than the one he's already carried out."

"I'll catch him," Montalbano replied calmly.

He'd held up pretty well in Pasquano's office, but as soon as he saw a bar, he stopped, got out of the car, and knocked back a cognac. He really needed it. Then he headed for the station.

"Ahh Chief Chief!"

"What is it?"

"Your collie called Seminario by the name o' Seminario called tree times! 'E says as how 'e's gotta talk t'yiz straight-aways emergently!"

"And you're going to tell him you can't find me."

"An' wha' if 'e reports it t'a'a C'mishner?"

"He won't, don't worry. Where's Fazio?"

"Jess got back."

"Send him to me."

He wanted to get out of there as quickly as possible. He was worried he might get roped into something at the last minute that would prevent him from being free at eight-thirty.

Fazio appeared.

"Did you get it?"

"I got everything."

"Sit down and talk."

Fazio was going to have his long-awaited revenge, a revenge years in the making. Settling into the chair, he wasted a little time properly adjusting his trousers, stuck a hand in his pocket, extracted a sheet of paper folded in two, looked at it as if he'd never seen it before, opened it, and smoothed it out. All very slowly. Then he looked Montalbano in the eye and, seeing that his boss was keeping quiet so as not to give him the satisfaction, he smiled triumphantly and started reading.

"Pennisi, first name Arturo, son of Carlo Pennisi and Alessandra Cavazzone, born in Montelusa on September 12, 1988, unmarried, legally a resident of Montelusa at number 129, Via Gioeni, but domiciled in Vigàta at 21, Via Bixio, in a house belonging to his maternal grandfather, Girolamo Cavazzone. Currently enrolled at the University of Palermo as a student in the department of—"

"Wait a second. Does Via Bixio by any chance run parallel to Via dei Mille?"

"Yessir. But the part of the street higher up, by the cemetery, actually leads directly into Via dei Mille."

The wild beast always moves on familiar ground.

"Now fold up that piece of paper and put it back in your pocket. You've gotten enough out of your system for now, I'd say."

Fazio obeyed. He'd had his revenge, after all, and with that extra sprinkle of sugar on it, it was sweet.

18

"Wha'd you say his grandfather's name was?"

"Cavazzone, first name Girolamo."

"Where have I heard that name before?"

And suddenly there was light: Girolamo Cavazzone!

The shabbily dressed, eighty-year-old albino, nephew of Gregorio Palmisano, the one who'd come to ask whether the Palmisanos, having been certified as insane, could be considered to all intents and purposes dead, so he could get his hands on the inheritance!

This was the final, missing link, the unhoped-for connection that dispelled all the inspector's remaining doubts. It closed the circle perfectly, sealing it shut.

Arturo had surely found the inflatable doll in his grandfather's attic; and surely Gregorio and Girolamo, when they still spoke, had bought two exactly the same.

This was what had enabled Arturo to do a test run on the doll that he later threw into the dumpster. Otherwise there would be no telling how or where he might find one.

The inspector stood up, smiling, walked around the desk and came to a stop right in front of Fazio, who was looking at him with a bewildered expression.

"Stand up."

Fazio obeyed, and Montalbano embraced him.

"Thanks for everything. You can go now."

Fazio didn't move, but only stared at him as though wanting to bore a hole through his eyes.

"Chief, what's going through your head?"

"Nothing. Why?"

"Then why did you want to know about that kid?"

"Look, it's something totally insubstantial, a pure fantasy. I'm going to do a little check tonight. If there's anything to it, I'll let you know. All right?"

Fazio went out, still doubtful.

To eat or not to eat? That was the question.

Not eating beforehand might mean not eating again until lunchtime the following day; eating right away would mean doing it far too early and hurriedly.

He decided against it. He remained seated on the veranda, smoking one cigarette after another, trying not to think about what he should do. In the end he concluded that it was best to have no plan of action at all and just wing it on the spot, depending on how the situation unfolded.

At twenty past eight, the phone rang.

"He's just rung the buzzer," said Ingrid. "He's waiting outside."

"All right."

"Don't forget that you have two hours, and not a minute more."

Before starting out, he made sure he had his more powerful flashlight in the car. Then he took his revolver out of the glove compartment and put it in his jacket pocket. The set of picklocks and skeleton keys a retired burglar friend had once given him lay on the passenger's seat beside him. He drove off.

The game of truth had just begun.

———

He had no trouble finding Via Nino Bixio. When he pulled up in front of a two-story house with the number 21 in front, it was five minutes to nine. The house had a little garden in front and an iron fence around it, but only in front. The inspector circled around the house in his car. There were two entrances in back: a small wooden door, perhaps a service entrance, and another larger one sealed shut behind a remote-controlled rolling shutter. That had to be the garage, which must lead in some way to the living area.

Arturo hadn't needed to take Ninetta out of the car to bring her inside. He'd slipped straight into the garage with the SUV and then could do whatever he wanted without being seen.

Just to be sure, Montalbano went around one more time. This time he noticed that on the front of the house, at ground level, there were four windows with iron gratings over them.

So there must be also a spacious cellar as large as the foundations of the building itself.

It wasn't a good idea to enter the house through the front door. There were too many cars driving by on Via Bixio. Better to use the little door in back, since the street it gave onto, Via Tukory, was much calmer.

He parked, got out of the car, fired up a cigarette, started walking like someone moseying around with nothing to do. He stopped briefly in front of the little door and had a look at the lock. It was one of those simple locks you open with a long key. A picklock should make pretty quick work of it.

He waited until there were no more cars passing, checked to make sure there was no one looking out of the windows of the houses opposite, pulled out his set of keys, and on the third try found the right one, opened the door, went inside, closed the door behind him, and lit his flashlight.

It took him three minutes to realize he'd got it all wrong. He'd entered a big room that must have once been a storeroom and was now a dump for things no longer needed: chairs without legs, worm-eaten furniture, chests of drawers . . . And worst of all, the storeroom was not connected with the living area.

Montalbano consoled himself with a couple of curses, turned off the flashlight, reopened the door, went out, and closed the door. There was no getting around it: willy-nilly, he would have to come in through the gate and the front door. And so he walked back around the house and returned to Via Bixio.

He glanced at his watch. Twenty past nine. His fuckup with the wrong door had cost him too much time, and he didn't have much to spare.

And there were still too many cars driving by. It was really the only problem, since the road was wide enough that the houses opposite presented no danger.

He decided that the wisest course was to wait another ten minutes or so. Around nine-thirty the flow of traffic should let up a bit.

Ten minutes later, he had the front gate open in a flash. The main door, however, immediately gave him trouble and, to top it off, a car pulled up in front of the house next door, catching him square in the glare of its headlights.

Then the car left, and a minute later the door let itself be coaxed open.

Lighting his way with the flashlight, he began to explore.

On the ground floor there was a dining room, a kitchen with a door leading to the basement, a small bathroom, and a living room. All in perfect order.

Directly opposite the door was a fine staircase leading upstairs. Montalbano went up. A very large bedroom, a fancy bathroom, a small study, and another room, locked. But not with the usual sort of lock you put on an inside door; this was a Yale lock and had been put in place rather recently. Which meant that there must be something very important in that room.

It took him another ten minutes to get it open, but he immediately realized that he hadn't wasted his time. It was another bedroom with a double bed with only a mattress, over which had been spread a large sheet of cellophane, now crumpled and stained. With blood.

There was a nightstand beside the bed with an empty glass on top. The window had been walled up from the inside, and the walls were all covered, like the inside of the door, with slabs of Styrofoam about seven inches thick, to make the room soundproof. The stale air in there stank unbearably of sweat, sperm, piss, and blood. In the corner, a broom. The upper end of the handle was dark. Montalbano went and got a better look at it. Clotted blood. Pasquano was right.

A cold shudder suddenly came over him, and he felt like throwing up but managed to hold back.

On the floor, pieces of brown adhesive tape, the kind used for packaging, and a still full roll.

It was clear that as soon as he'd kidnapped Ninetta, he brought her in here and made her drink the poison that killed her.

But he hadn't disfigured her in there. The bloodstains on the cellophane were too small. No, she was already dead when he laid her down on that bed to use her as he would an inflatable doll. The bloody broomstick was proof of that.

Montalbano left the room, closed the door, and went into the bathroom to wash his face. But he didn't want to use the towel. He found it too disgusting. A faint sort of current was running through his whole body, and he was trembling slightly all over. He went into the study, which was stuffed with books. On the desk was a computer, a Polaroid camera, and a cardboard box, which he opened. There were dozens of photographs inside.

The first photos his eye fell on showed Ninetta laid out on the bed fully clothed, but with her mouth sealed with the same tape in which her wrists and ankles were bound. Other photos showed the rubber doll that she'd been turned into, with legs spread, or variously, on her tummy. The remainder documented the gradual transformation her corpse had been subjected to.

Montalbano put them in his jacket pocket. Those photos were more than enough to screw Arturo. He could leave now.

He looked at his watch. Ten-twenty-five. He realized that, assuming Ingrid's and Arturo's dinner ended at ten-thirty sharp, the kid would still take at least fifteen minutes to get home.

He went downstairs, into the kitchen, and opened the door. Five broad steps led down to the cellar.

A large room with only four old barrels and a great many dust-covered wall shelves that had once served to hold bottles of wine. And there was a door, which he opened.

And here everything changed. In the middle of the room there was a proper operating table, all covered with blood, with a small table on wheels beside it. On this were a spoon, an awl, several rolls of adhesive bandage, two large rolls of the same packaging tape, a razor, a glass of water with something bloody inside it, probably Ninetta's eye. In one corner were a pair of shoes and some woman's clothing. The girl's. In another corner, a plastic garbage can. But it was full of blood. The blood Arturo had drained from her body before painting her up.

And near the operating table, another small table with a video screen and a disc player. By some miracle the inspector managed to make it work. On the screen appeared the images of Gregorio Palmisano's inflatable doll that had been broadcast on TeleVigàta. Apparently Arturo had wanted the recording ready at hand, first for practicing on his grandfather's doll, and then to work on Ninetta's body.

But there was another door, and Montalbano opened it. This third room was smaller than the other two. Here, too, the window was walled up from the inside. On two small tables sat at least four computers and other electronic equipment whose exact purpose wasn't clear to the inspector. What was certain, however, was that it was with this setup that Arturo had downloaded and printed all the still shots with which he had papered the walls of the wooden shack.

There was nothing else to see.

He turned around to leave, and in the beam of the flashlight saw Arturo standing in the doorway with a pistol in his hand.

Montalbano felt paralyzed. He realized he was trapped, unable to react in the slightest way, since Arturo could empty his whole magazine into him without anyone outside hearing anything.

But what most struck the inspector, much more than the gun pointed at him, was Arturo's attitude. The kid didn't seem the least bit scared, nervous, or worried. At the most, you could say he looked a little annoyed.

He turned on the light and said:

"Please sit down."

Montalbano sat down in the first chair within reach. Arturo grabbed another.

"How are you doing?" the youth asked.

"Not too bad," said the inspector.

The guy was truly a dangerous psychopath. What would he do next, offer him a cup of tea?

"It was you who told Ingrid to invite me out to dinner, wasn't it?"

"Yes."

There was no reason to lie to him.

"I'm very intelligent, you know. I caught on after a while and was able to get rid of her."

Montalbano became alarmed.

"What do you mean, 'get rid of her'?"

Harry Potter flashed a knowing smile, like a sly child. That smile made Montalbano's blood run cold. Want to bet the guy quite sincerely considered the murder and butchery of Ninetta's body just a game? A boyish prank? Want to bet that his form of homicidal madness was a kind of unconscious infantile cruelty? Like cutting off the tails of lizards?

"Don't worry," said Arturo, using the familiar form of address. "She's back at home, safe and sound. While we were in the car, she tried twice to call out on her cell phone, but didn't get through. Maybe she was trying to warn you."

"So, what do we do now?" Montalbano asked.

"I'm thinking it over. Meanwhile, let's chat a little, what do you say?"

"Why not?"

"How did you figure out I was your challenger in the treasure hunt?"

"I thought back on the things you said and wrote to me. You made one slip of the tongue and two omissions. Three mistakes. Too many."

Upon hearing this reply, Arturo's face was transformed. His mouth twisted up, his eyes frowned, a deep furrow appeared on his brow. He stood up and started stamping his feet.

"No! No! No! I don't make mistakes! You are a lot less intelligent than me! At the most, you might be a little more shrewd! Damn you!"

Lightning fast, he struck him square in the face with the gun.

Montalbano's nose started bleeding.

"Can I take out my handkerchief?"

"No!"

So Montalbano bent his head back as far as it would go, hoping the bleeding would stop promptly. He was more than ever convinced that murdering Ninetta had dealt the final blow to the kid's already damaged brain.

Until now he'd always been able to hide his madness, but

now it was visible in every move he made. After a few minutes, Montalbano was able to speak again.

"Can I ask you a question?"

"I don't want to hear it."

He was pouting, the boy. Just like a child.

"Come on, just one."

"Oh, all right."

"Did you kidnap Ninetta because you already knew her, or because she looked like that girl from the brothel?"

"I wanted the girl from the brothel. But I just couldn't find her. And so I stole an SUV and started looking for someone who looked like her. Then, when I was passing a bus, I saw a girl that I thought was her. But when I stopped and pretended to ask her for directions, she came forward and I realized she wasn't the girl I was looking for, but the resemblance was stunning. And so I grabbed her."

"Can I ask you two more questions?"

"And then that's all?"

"And then that's all."

"Swear it."

"I swear it. Where did you find the inflatable doll?"

"Here. In the attic. It was my grandfather's."

He'd been right on the money.

"And the lamb's head, how'd you do it?"

"That was pretty good, eh?"

"No doubt about it."

"I was driving around near Gallotta and I saw an untended flock, so I grabbed a lamb, slit its throat, stuck it in the trunk, brought it here, cut its head off and put it in an old cookie tin that was in the attic. And now no more questions."

"What are you going to do?"

The youth began to stare at him thoughtfully, tapping the barrel of the gun lightly against his lips. Then he made up his mind.

"Let's go in the other room. You first."

Montalbano would never manage to pull out his revolver in time; the kid would have all the time in the world to shoot first. He stood up and went into the other room.

"Stop in front of the bed."

That was the last thing he heard but one. The very last thing was the powerful crash of the pistol butt against his head, which knocked him out.

He opened his eyes. The back of his head hurt like hell. He was lying on the operating table, stripped down to his underpants, mouth, wrists, and ankles immobilized with duct tape. His clothes lay on top of Ninetta's. The door of the room was closed. He realized that his only hope for saving his skin was to keep the kid talking. But how could he do that with his mouth taped shut? He couldn't. He was finished. And at that moment, as though projecting himself out of his body, he saw himself there, in his underpants, socks, and shoes, lying on an operating table, and he found himself so ridiculous that he started laughing.

He was laughing because his brain refused to accept what was happening to him. It was the kind of thing you might see in a horror film or some fantasy movie, not in real life.

He heard a key turn, and the door opened.

Arturo had returned with a chain saw, a hammer, and a chisel. What the fuck was the kid thinking? Maybe he wanted to play surgeon. He extracted from his pocket one of those steel boxes for syringes and set it down on one of the small tables, next to his pistol.

"I'll explain," he said. "I want to have a good look at your brain. I want to examine it up close, *live*. Understand? And so I have to remove the top of your skull. But I'll put you to sleep first."

Montalbano, drenched in sweat, tried to control the panic that was taking hold of him. He howled.

"Did you want to say something?"

Montalbano nodded yes, shaking his head up and down desperately. The kid tore off the tape, causing him pain.

"What is it?"

"I wanted to suggest another game. A fantastic game. Something that'll require your full intelligence."

For a second, Arturo's eyes sparkled with contentment.

"Really?!"

"Yes, you'll see."

Then suddenly the kid's eyes darkened.

"I don't believe you. Anyway, we don't need to play another game to prove that I can beat you every time."

And he taped the inspector's mouth back up.

Montalbano's only hope was that the anesthesia would actually work.

Arturo grabbed the metal box, opened it, took out a syringe, and with his other hand he pulled out a little phial, filled the syringe, and then checked it against the light for air bubbles.

Montalbano closed his eyes.

And he thought he'd fallen asleep in the twinkling of an eye, because it wasn't possible that what he was hearing was the cool, calm voice of Fazio.

"Freeze right there, little asshole. Make the slightest move and I'll kill you."

He opened his eyes. It was true!

Fazio had his gun trained on Arturo, who looked like he'd turned into a statue. Behind Fazio were Gallo and Galluzzo, who in the space of ten seconds jumped on the kid, slammed him to the ground, and handcuffed him.

"Why? Why?" Arturo wailed, his voice on the verge of tears. "We were just playing. . . ."

Without understanding why, Montalbano felt a heartbreaking sorrow.

Fazio, meanwhile, had come up to him and was delicately removing the tape from his mouth. The first thing the inspector asked was:

"Who alerted you?"

"Signora Ingrid. She told me you'd asked her to keep the kid away from his house for a while, but she got scared that it was maybe too early. And so I called Gallo and Galluzzo and came straight here. You told me yourself you were going to do a little check."

"Call Seminara at once. Then pass me the cell phone so I can tell Ingrid everything's all right."

When he got home to Marinella it was almost three in the morning. He was so famished he could have eaten a live elephant. Inside the oven he found a large casserole of *pasta 'ncasciata* and eight *arancini*, each one bigger than a real orange. As he headed for the bathroom to take a shower, he started singing out loud. As off-key as a church bell. And when he was done eating, he very nearly had to drag himself to the telephone to call Livia, though the sun was already rising, and tell her that he'd be flying to Genoa that very day.

Author's Note

Everything in this novel, names and surnames, situations and events, is only the fruit of my imagination. If anyone should recognize himself in one of my characters, it means he has more imagination than I.

Notes

5 a municipal cop: That is, what Italians call a *vigile urbano*, who is under a different jurisdiction from the *commissariato*, which Montalbano is chief of, and which handles criminal investigations.

29 having a few cats to comb: A literal translation of the Sicilian expression, which means to have tedious, difficult, and useless chores to attend to.

63 *spaghetti alle vongole veraci* (and truly *veraci*): *Vongole* of course are clams, but the dish is generally served with either one of two species of small clams: *telline*, which are the smaller variety, with smooth, shiny shells; and the *vongole veraci*, the "real" *vongole*, which are larger, with striated shells, and more savory and prized.

74 "pewters": Catarella's word for "computers."

90 *Settimana Enigmistica:* An immensely popular Italian weekly of puzzles including rebuses, acrostics, crossword puzzles, and riddles, created in 1932.

109 *cuddriruni:* A kind of Sicilian focaccia.

126 *cacio all'argintera:* Caciocavallo cheese sliced fine and sautéed in olive oil with garlic, oregano, vinegar, and a pinch of sugar and salt.

231 *Ex ore tuo te judico:* By thine own mouth will I judge thee (Luke 19:22).

273 *arancini:* Traditional Sicilian fried rice balls. Literally "little oranges," *arancini* are normally considerably smaller than the ones Adelina has made for Montalbano.

Notes by Stephen Sartarelli